SUPERIORS

SUPERIORS

Donald Sossamon

To order additional copies of this book, contact:
Xlibris
844-714-8691
www.Xlibris.com
Orders@Xlibris.com
827403

SUPERIORS

EXT. CLOUDY OPEN AREA - DAY

Louis, a young looking angel with feathered wings, kneels.

Two other angels, Fredrick, and Anthony, walk up and kneel near Louis...

The three angels wear light blue metal body armor.

A portal opens behind them.

The portal swirls with light blue and gray colors.

> DEEP VOICE
> New souls will turn to Angels...
> Heaven and Hell must be balanced...

The three angels stand and look at the portal...

INT. LOUIS' CABIN - BEDROOM - DAY

SUPER: 1797

The bedroom is small and plain...

Louis wakes up suddenly on his bed wearing a night cap, and gown. He shakes his head for a moment, then gets out of bed.

EXT. BARBER STAND - STREET - DAY

Louis helps a barber at an outdoor shop on a street corner...

He wears a cravat, with a shirt, coat and breeches.

His hair is long and tied back.

He grabs the Barber's tools and puts them in a water bucket.

The barber, John 50, starts taking down surrounding drapes.

> JOHN
> How about you let me cut your hair? You can
> get yourself a nice wig after...

> LOUIS
> Sure... Alright...

Louis unties his hair and sits down in a chair.

John puts an apron on him, and starts to cut his hair.

Louis shuts his eyes in pain.

John grabs another strand and chops.

Louis opens his eyes and both eyeballs briefly glow blue, before going back to normal.

He groans and quickly stands.

> JOHN
> Sorry! Did I cut you?

Louis' hair grows back and his finger nails, and his teeth grow long and sharp.

JOHN
What on Earth!?

Louis looks at John for a moment, and runs off...

As he runs he turns back to normal...

EXT. LOUIS' CABIN - NIGHT

Three men wearing quaker attire, Silas, 45 years old, Terrance, 48, and Abraham, 40, approach a medium size log cabin in a forest area.

Terrance carries a torch and they all have a sword holstered on their belts.

Silas stops suddenly...

Terrance and Abraham stop and look at Silas...

ABRAHAM
What is it Silas?

SILAS
Something does not feel right...

TERRANCE
Silas, this has to be done. Now let us go.

The three men walk up to the door and Terrance pounds on it.

INT. LOUIS' CABIN - FRONT ROOM - SAME

Louis approaches the door wearing breeches and a shirt.

>   TERRANCE
>   (from outside)
> We have heard from the townsfolk that you
> transformed into a beast before the barber's eyes!

EXT. CABIN - FRONT DOOR - SAME

>   TERRANCE
>   Surrender yourself!

There is a loud slam from the side of the cabin.

The three quakers run to the side of the cabin and see Louis on the ground below a window.

Louis stands up and starts fleeing.

The quakers chase him.

Terrance rushes up to Louis, and Louis turns around and grabs the torch from Terrance.

He kicks Terrance in the stomach and rips the torch from him.

His eyes glow blue, and his teeth and nails become sharp...

He drops the torch on the ground and it stays lit and lights the area around them...

Silas rushes up and draws his sword.

He swings at Louis, and Louis twists, and evades.

Abraham runs up and pulls out his sword.

Louis grabs it from him with his right hand, and hits Abraham in the face with his left elbow, causing him to fall.

Louis yanks the sword from Abraham's hand as he falls...

Silas swings again at Louis, and he blocks...

They press their swords against each other...

Louis holds his sword still as Silas presses against him... After a moment he pushes his sword forward, and knocks Silas down...

He throws the sword on the ground, looks at his claws for a moment, then rushes up to Terrance and slashes his chest...

Terrance groans, turns and falls...

Abraham stands and rushes Louis, and Louis slashes Abraham in his stomach and chest.

Silas stands and Louis runs over and thrusts his claws into his stomach...

Silas looks in Louis' eyes...

QUICK FLASH

EXT. CLOUDY OPEN AREA - DAY

Louis, Fredrick, and Anthony look at the swirling portal...

It swirls with light blue and gray colors.

They all jump in...

BACK TO:

EXT. FORREST AREA - NIGHT

Louis pulls his hands out of Silas' stomach and Silas groans and falls.

Louis looks around and runs away...

Terrance, Abraham and Silas rise from the ground...

Their eyes open, and their wounds glow bright green.

Louis turns around and watches as the wounds on the three men heal, and wings of flesh and bone grow, and rip out of their back.

Fangs grow in their mouth, and their nails grow long and sharp.

Their wounds get unusually infected because of Louis' claw attacks, and they become the first vampires ever on Earth...

Louis starts to run faster into the woods as Terrance and Abraham both leap into the air and fly toward him...

Terrance and Abraham land, and charge Louis.

Silas flies up to Abraham and Terrance...

                    SILAS
          Wait!

Terrance slashes Louis in the chest with his claws and Louis falls.

Abraham rushes Louis and slashes his throat...

Silas kneels near Louis and grabs his hand as he chokes...

                    SILAS
          I told you it did not feel right...

                    TERRANCE
What do you mean? He's a demon Silas. Look
what he did.

                    SILAS
We did not have to kill him.

Louis dies...

Silas closes his eyes and has a vision...

QUICK FLASH

EXT. PORTAL - DAY

The angels, Louis, Fredrick, and Anthony fly through the swirling
portal...

                                              BACK TO:

EXT. FORREST AREA - NIGHT

                    ABRAHAM
What's going on Silas?...

                    SILAS
I was shown something... I think I received a
vision... This man was not a demon... he was
actually an angel before he came to Earth...

QUICK FLASH

INT. LARGE COLORFUL AREA - BENCH - DAY/NIGHT

Louis lies on the ground next to a light blue bench.

He wakes up in a strange area that is mainly dark gray everywhere, but has constant colorful ink blot looking orbs coming and going everywhere.

The colors are turquoise, silver, and green...

He gets up and looks around for a moment before sitting on the bench and leaning his head on his hands...

BACK TO:

EXT. FORREST AREA - NIGHT

Silas, Terrance, and Abraham stand around Louis' dead body.

Silas' chest twitches and he quickly grabs a small cross around his neck as it burns his chest...

Smoke comes from his chest and his fingers start to burn.

The crosses on Terrance and Abraham's chest start to burn them as well...

The three vampires rip the crosses from their necks and toss them on the ground.

> TERRANCE
> What does this mean!?

> SILAS
> I don't know... but the lord may be trying to tell
> us that what we did was wrong...

EXT. FORREST AREA - DAY

The men walk on a path near small mountains, and hills...

The sun starts to come out and burns Silas, Terrance, and Abraham...

The men quickly run into a small cave on a mountainside...

TERRANCE
The Sun... It's burning us...

ABRAHAM
Is The Lord abandoning us Silas?

Silas pauses and closes his eyes...

TERRANCE
Silas, is The Lord trying to kill
us?...

QUICK FLASH

INT. UNDERGROUND CAVE AREA - NIGHT

Silas has a vision of a large open underground area...

BACK TO:

INT. SMALL MOUNTAINSIDE CAVE - DAY

Silas looks at the other two vampires...

SILAS
I do not believe we have been abandoned... We
attacked that man, and now we may be cursed
for it... but we are not damned... We must
continue to serve The Lord.

EXT. SKY - NIGHT

The sun is just behind the mountains and Silas, Terrance, and Abraham fly over a forest area.

Silas carries a shovel, Terrance carries a pick axe, and Abraham carries a wood axe.

Silas suddenly stops midair, and the other two stop as well.

The three vampires land on the ground, and walk to a mountain where there is a waterfall, and a large tree to the side...

Terrance and Abraham start to smash into the ground between the tree and the waterfall, as Silas shovels debris.

After a moment the ground gives way and they fall...

They quickly recover in a spherical tunnel.

Terrance looks back and forth in both directions.

>   ABRAHAM
>   Right where you said Silas...

Silas nods...

>   SILAS
>   Come on, this way.

Silas begins to walk in one direction of the tunnel...

>   TERRANCE
>   What is the other way Silas?

>   SILAS
>   It just goes and goes... Nowhere we need worry
>   about now.

They continue to walk...

EXT. UNDERGROUND CAVE - OPEN AREA - NIGHT

After a moment, they reach a large open area in the cave.

Some moonlight comes from cracks in the mountain above.

> SILAS
> We are to build a church and swear to preserve
> it... for us, and for whomever we turn.

EXT. UNDERGROUND CAVE - NIGHT

SUPER: ONE YEAR LATER

In the large open area, there is now a wooden church, and

bright moonlight shines through the cracks of the cave...

INT. UNDERGROUND CHURCH - MAIN HALL - NIGHT

At the altar, Terrance reads from a bible...

Silas, Abraham, and twenty other vampires sit in the pews listening...

Half of them have wings and the others do not...

> TERRANCE
> We do not wrestle with the living... but against
> the spiritual and the physical forces of evil that
> attack heavenly places...

Silas holds a closed bible and closes his eyes...

White light comes from the cracks of his closed eyes...

INT. UNDERGROUND CHURCH - SMALL ROOM - NIGHT

A woman, Angela 20, lies on a table, squirming and screaming.

Silas, and another vampire, Nicholas, eternally 30, stand near her...

Silas walks towards Angela stunned... Veins on her neck pop out and turn red...

The whites in her eyes start to turn red...

                    NICHOLAS
          What happened Silas?

                    SILAS
          A demon overlord is possessing her... If I turn
          her it may counter the possession... It is the only
          thing I can do...

                    ANGELA
          Do it!

Silas' fangs grow long as he leans in and bites her neck.

Angela screams for a moment... then slowly, she becomes calm.

Silas holds out his arm, pulls a small sword from a waist holster, and cuts his arm.

                    SILAS
          Drink dear...

Silas holds his arm above her, and she sits up, grabs him and drinks his blood...

NICHOLAS
Is it going to work Silas?...

SILAS
I do not know...

Angela lays back down...

She lets out an animalistic roar... After a moment she catches herself, closes her eyes, and breathes slowly...

INT. UNDERGROUND CHURCH - SMALL BEDROOM - NIGHT

Silas sleeps on a basic wooden bed in a small room... Above him, a young looking female angel floats...

She leans in close to his ear and whispers...

ANGEL
You have turned enough for now...
Continue to feed, but do not turn another... If
you do... they will be given the power by God
to destroy you all.

SILAS
I understand...

EXT. ALLEY - NIGHT

Matthew, 30, walks wearing a cravat and jacket.

Nicholas jumps down from a rooftop, wraps his arm around Matthew, and bites him.

Matthew tenses up, groans, and backs into a wall... He quickly grabs Nicholas by the hand and bites him.

NICHOLAS
No! Stop!

With his thumb claw, Nicholas slices Matthew's throat and runs away.

Matthew drops, as his mouth drips Nicholas' blood...

He coughs and quickly checks his throat... His wound begins to heal...

Matthew wipes the blood on his mouth, and neck, and shakes his head...

Fangs grow in Matthew's mouth and his eyes shoot out bright white light... after a moment the light mellows...

The mild white light in his eyes shines blue for a moment, then he glares ahead at Nicholas running...

Matthew shuts his eyes... focuses... and hears Nicholas' footsteps...

He opens his eyes and the blue light shines red for a moment before his eyes go back to normal...

INT. UNDERGROUND CHURCH - NIGHT

Nicholas walks into the church...

He walks through the front room of the church as several vampires enter the sanctuary, from the basement.

SANCTUARY AREA

The vampires sit in the pews.

Silas and Abraham stand at the altar...

Anna, eternally 35, and Charles, eternally 40, stand near Silas and Abraham...

The pews all have long staff-like posts at the ends.

Nicholas sits and grabs a bible.

The doors to the sanctuary burst open and Matthew walks in.

Nicholas looks at Matthew...

Matthew notices Nicholas, and quickly starts charging towards him...

A group of vampires stand and rush towards Matthew.

Vampires surround him and he stops...

Matthew rips out a post connected to a pew, breaks it in half, and stabs it into the nearest male vampire's chest.

Another male vampire, Vampire Man #2 edges close to Matthew.

Matthew stabs Vampire Man #2 in the chest, pushes through the crowd, hops over a pew and launches himself onto Nicholas.

He starts stabbing Nicholas repeatedly with the post.

The entire crowd of vampires circle around Matthew...

A woman vampire, Female Vampire #1, slashes Matthew's shoulder and Matthew groans...

After a moment, his wound heals.

Matthew turns and stabs the Female Vampire #1 in the chest.

Matthew looks at his nails and they turn to claws...

ON SILAS

Abraham and Silas look at Matthew in shock...

Terrance walks in from a back room, looks at Matthew and pauses...

On the wall of the altar, there are swords, spears, and shields.

Terrance and Anna grab swords, and Abraham and Charles both grab spears.

ON MATTHEW

Matthew continues to attack the vampires in the crowd.

Vampires rush Matthew and he hops over pews to an open area.

A male vampire, Vampire Man #3, tries to rush toward Matthew and Matthew stabs him in the side of the throat with the post and leaves it in him.

Another male, Vampire Man #4, grabs a sword from the altar, charges Matthew, and swings at him.

Matthew ducks, drives his claws through Vampire Man #4's chin, and grabs his sword...

He stabs a male vampire, Vampire Man#5, in the chest with the sword...

Matthew claws a female vampire, Female Vampire #2, in the throat.

He throws his sword in the chest of another charging male vampire, Vampire Man #6...

Abraham rushes and stabs Matthew in the chest with his spear.

He pushes the spear further into Matthew's heart...

Anna and Abraham smile and pause for a moment...

Matthew drops his sword and pulls the spear out of his chest.

His chest and heart heal, and he throws the spear at Abraham, and it stabs him in the chest.

Charles and Anna charge Matthew.

Matthew rips the spear from Charles' hands, smacks him in the head with it, and stabs him in the heart.

Anna runs up and slashes toward Matthew and he evades.

He kicks her in the chest, and she slams on the floor, and drops her sword...

Matthew quickly grabs Anna's sword from the ground and a male vampire, Vampire Man #7, claws Matthew's chest.

Matthew's chest heals and he decapitates Vampire Man #7...

Matthew turns to Anna and stabs her in the neck and pulls out the sword.

Matthew approaches Terrance, who is stunned...

> MATTHEW
> I know what all of you creatures are... I have heard the stories from the townsfolk. They call you vampires...

> TERRANCE
> We all serve The Lord here. We were told about you... Someone must have disobeyed the rules set before us...

MATTHEW

Quiet! The people say you are all some kind of...
cursed demons!...

Terrance throws his sword down and gets closer.

TERRANCE

I am no demon. I mean you no harm.

MATTHEW

Quiet! Do not lie to me!

SILAS

Terrance!

Terrance closes his eyes and Matthew decapitates him.

MATTHEW

Why did you creatures have to turn me into
one of you!?

Silas walks up to Matthew.

SILAS

I do not know what happened to you, but you
did not have to do this.

MATTHEW

Make peace with your God demon.

SILAS

Hold on... You can trust me... I am shown
things...

Matthew puts the sword near Silas' neck.

SILAS

Foresight!... Incredible intuition!... Wait! I was told by an angel that we were not supposed to turn another... That's why you were given more power!...

They calm down...

MATTHEW

You see? I was supposed to do this...

SILAS

It is not about destiny... Let me explain to you what I know...

Matthew lowers his sword...

MATTHEW

What do you mean?...

SILAS

You were given this power, this, extra strength to defeat us... but the future is never set. You didn't have to do this...

MATTHEW

You mean I could have ruled you all instead?

SILAS

If that's what you wanted to do... however... if you really want to use your power to destroy demons, you and I could do that.

MATTHEW

No!... All of you cursed must die.

Matthew swings to chop...

Silas quickly waves an amber colored mist in Matthew's face.

Matthew gets the mist in his eyes and pauses...

After a moment he lowers the sword, and looks at all of the dead vampires...

>   MATTHEW
>   Very well... We shall allow The Lord to guide us...

Silas stands...

>   SILAS
>   You must pray for guidance as well.

Matthew pauses for a moment, then nods...

INT. UNDERGROUND CHURCH - MATTHEW'S BEDROOM - NIGHT

In the room there is a small bed and a candle lit on a night stand.

Matthew sleeps and Silas stands above him, waving his hands near his head while amber mist trickles down.

Silas blows out the candle and walks out of the room.

INT. UNDERGROUND CHURCH - MAIN HALL - NIGHT

Silas sits near the alter reading a Bible.

Matthew comes in from another room and walks up to Silas.

MATTHEW
I believe I've had a vision, like you... I know
where to find demons.

SILAS
Good... So let's go then.

EXT. STREET - NIGHT

Silas and Matthew walk down a rainy street as a large horse drawn
carriage passes by...

They turn down into an alley and approach a basement door on the
ground, and they both open it...

INT. BASEMENT AREA - NIGHT

Silas and Matthew walk down a stone hall to a wooden door guarded
by Cid, 35...

Cid is tall with a muscular build and wears a frontiersman's outfit.

CID
What do you two want?

Silas pulls out a calvary saber from a holster and swings at Cid.

Cid ducks and kicks Silas, and Silas flies back...

Cid's eyes turn black with red pupils.

Cid pulls a one handed axe from a back holster and swings at Matthew.

Matthew ducks and punches Cid in the back of the neck.

Silas runs up to Cid and Cid quickly grabs Silas' throat.

Matthew pulls out a long tactical knife and swings at Cid.

Cid lets go of Silas, and spins out of the way.

He chops at Matthew and he blocks and kicks Cid in the side.

Cid drops to his knees and Matthew stabs his neck...

Silas and Matthew kick open the wooden door and inside is a small pub, with three tables.

There are two demon men and one women...

Dem Man#1, Dem Man#2, and Dem Woman#1, sit at a table.

The bartender, Dem Man#3 stands behind the bar.

Dem Man#3 grabs a derringer pistol, hops over the bar and shoots Silas in the chest.

All of the demons eyes turn black...

Matthew throws his knife into Dem Man#3's stomach.

Silas recovers, and looks at his wound as it heals.

Dem Man#1 runs up and swings at Matthew.

Matthew spins, and stabs Dem Man#1 in the chest.

Dem Man#2 runs up and grabs Silas by his shirt.

Dem Women#1 pulls out a small knife and swings at Matthew.

Matthew evades a slash, and a chop.

He grabs her arm, breaks it, slashes her throat with his claws, and then bites her neck.

Silas headbutts Dem Man#2, grabs his wrists and jump kicks him with both feet...

Matthew runs up and drives his claws in Dem Man#2's stomach.

Matthew looks around, then at Silas...

Silas nods to Matthew.

EXT. VOLCANO - OPENING ON TOP - NIGHT

Silas and Matthew stand on a cliff that is on the side of a volcano.

Smoke comes from the volcano as a large creature crawls out of it...

The creature is Mammon, a large demon, 7'4, wearing black armor that covers his chest... The skin on his arms, legs, and neck looks like thick dry lava... His hands and wrists are charcoal colored, and are as solid as stone. His face is covered in a helmet, and black horns come out of the top of his head. His heart is large and pokes out of his chest, and it is covered in a thick red skin.

Silas and Matthew both wear long overcoats and have each grown beards...

Matthew carries a thick one handed steel sword, and Silas has his calvary saber...

Silas stares at Mammon's heart for a moment...

MAMMON
Matthew... you are well known in hell.

Mammon's voice is low and intense...

Matthew chops at Mammon and he quickly blocks with his wrist.

Silas runs up, jumps, and thrusts his sword into Mammon's leg.

Mammon smacks Matthew with a backhand and he goes flying...

Silas looks over at Matthew...

Mammon swings at Silas and he ducks.

Silas rushes over to Matthew and helps him up...

Mammon approaches the two vampires...

Matthew recovers and they both rush Mammon...

Matthew swings at Mammon, and he blocks again with his wrist.

Silas swings a punch at Mammon's mid-section, and Mammon quickly blocks.

Matthew slashes up Mammon's chest.

Mammon kicks Matthew, and creates a fireball in his hand...

He throws the fireball at Matthew and it hits him, lighting him on fire...

SILAS
Matthew!

Matthew stands and Mammon hurls another fireball at him...

Matthew puts his arms together and blocks...

He quickly takes off his coat and hits himself with it to put out the fire...

Mammon kicks Silas knocking him back...

Matthew rushes Mammon...

Mammon swings at Matthew, and Matthew quickly dodges.

Matthew thrusts his sword into Mammon's collar bone.

Mammon front kicks Matthew, and Matthew holds onto his sword, as he goes flying...

He lands and his sword slips out of his hands...

He crawls quickly to the edge to try to catch his sword but it's too late and it falls off the cliff...

Silas charges Mammon and Mammon grabs Silas, throws him up, punches him, and Silas gets launched by the punch...

Mammon pulls out Silas' sword from his leg and throws it off the cliff.

Matthew looks at Silas, gets up and slowly walks towards Mammon.

Silas stands.

> MATTHEW
> Stay back Silas...

Matthew approaches Mammon...

> MAMMON
> A vampire that doesn't turn to ash when hit by
> fire? You truly are blessed...

Matthew squeezes his hands into a fist...

MAMMON
You don't get visions like him...
He lied to you.

MATTHEW
What?

MAMMON
Your are not gifted with divine cognition...
You can feel that he isn't to be trusted can't
you?... All those visions of demons... they were
put by him... He's been your suppressing your
potential, and keeping you occupied, so you
wont use your power for your own personal
gain.

SILAS
Matthew don't listen to him!

MAMMON
Join me, instead of fighting me...
We can focus on what YOU want to do with
your abilities...

MATTHEW
I wish to destroy demons...

MAMMON
No need. It may take some time, but I can help
you rule them instead...

Silas starts walking toward Matthew...

SILAS
Matthew! Wait!

Matthew looks at Silas...

> MATTHEW
> Leave Silas!...

> MAMMON
> Why should we let him live?

> MATTHEW
> He's no threat... He's weak...

Mammon crosses his arms and stares...

Silas looks at them for a moment, then jumps and flies away.

He flies through the sky for a moment, before looking back at Matthew and Mammon.

He looks forward, shakes his head, and continues on...

INT. CAVE - NIGHT

SUPER: 1986

Silas sleeps in a dark cave on a flat rock near a waterfall coming from a mountain above...

Moonlight shines down near the waterfall...

Silas wears denim pants, and a leather jacket...

He now has a Samurai sword holstered on his belt...

He squeezes his eyes tight and has a vision...

QUICK FLASH

INT. SNOWY CAVE - DAY

A frozen giant man lies on the ground, face down, wearing nothing but a loin cloth...

BACK TO:

INT. CAVE - NIGHT

Silas' eyes quickly open and he sits up straight on the rock for a moment...

EXT. SNOWY MOUNTAIN SIDE - DAY

It is early morning... snow falls and clouds block the sun.

Silas flies by a mountain side, and lands near the bottom.

He walks into a tall cave passage blocked by large icicles, pulls out his Samurai sword and slashes at the icicles.

He walks through a large, half frozen cave area...

After a moment he sees a tunneled out path and follows it.

He puts his sword away and pulls out a metal flashlight.

On the bottom of the flashlight, a tag reads "1979."

He notices a large, high vaulted room where the frozen giant from his vision lies on the ground.

> SILAS
> Well the bad news is, you, and all of your kind
> are nearly extinct.

Silas sets the flashlight down and pulls out his sword.

SILAS
Good news is... you wont feel this.

Silas chops off the giants hand.

EXT. MOUNTAIN SIDE - CAVE ENTRANCE - DAY

Silas walks out and stuffs the frozen hand in his jacket.

To his left stands Herman, 132 years old...

Herman is eight foot, ten inches tall and wears a long withered shirt...

Silas notices Herman, and Herman runs up and smacks Silas, sending him flying...

He lands and notices the frozen giant's hand on the ground.

He grabs the hand, stands up, and notices Herman running at him.

Herman punches Silas, and Silas slams against a tree.

Silas groans, still holding onto the frozen hand...

He gets up and starts to run...

He can hear the stomps of the giant behind him...

Silas turns around, and quickly pulls out his sword.

Herman swings his fist at Silas.

His fist goes right into Silas' sword but the skin barely cuts open, and only a small amount of blood drips...

Herman grabs Silas and punches him in the stomach, launching him away.

Silas lands, and sees the hand about ten feet away...

He stands, and looks at a tiny drop of blood on his sword...

> SILAS
> (to self)
> Is this enough?...

He sighs, and the giant starts running toward him...

Silas rushes to the hand, picks it up and flies off just before Herman gets to him...

EXT. MANSION - FRONT YARD - NIGHT

The property has a large lawn...

The front of the property is gated with a guard shack...

INT. GUARD SHACK - NIGHT

A guard, Lough, 50, sleeps in a chair, near a desk that has a security monitor on it...

EXT. MANSION - FRONT YARD - NIGHT

Near the front door, an old man, Jim Leti, 75, stands outside wearing a robe, and smoking a cigarette.

Silas comes down from the sky, and lands on the lawn.

Jim Leti doesn't budge, and continues to puff on his smoke as he looks at the vampire...

He looks over at the guard shack and shakes his head...

SILAS

Jim Leti?

JIM

Has my time come?

Jim throws his cigarette on the ground...

SILAS

Uh, No. That's not my modus operandi. There's
no need to fear me.

Silas pulls the giant hand wrapped in plastic, from his coat.

JIM

Your just gonna show me a huge, severed hand
on my front lawn?...

SILAS

I have a favor to ask. I believe you could
help me...

INT. MANSION - KITCHEN - NIGHT

Jim and Silas sit at the kitchen table...

The kitchen is large with a wall oven that has a flip clock.

JIM

I don't do this stuff Silas.

SILAS

Jim I know all about your achievements... I
know you could handle this... It should be easy.

                    JIM

So, you're telling me... you expect me to help genetically engineer a giant? I... don't know... I need a volunteer to start...

                    SILAS

Okay... Give me some time... I'll try to bring you one...

EXT. CABIN - FORREST AREA - DAY

The sun is almost completely down...

The Forrest area outside is mainly dirt and leaves with a few hills and mountains near.

Silas lands in the front yard of the property...

INT. CABIN - KITCHEN - SAME

A woman, Teri, 41, sits in her kitchen with a glass of tea.

On the stove there is chicken cooking on a pan and black beans in a pot...

She takes a sip of tea and grabs a picture on her table...

The picture is of her and a man, Jacob, 45, holding each other, near a lake.

She smiles while looking at the picture... after a moment she hears the chicken on the stove sizzle, and crackle.

She gets up and turns off both burners on the stove.

There is a knock at the front door...

She walks over and opens the door.

Silas stands on the porch.

Teri quickly grabs a baseball bat near the door.

> SILAS
>
> Don't be alarmed.

> TERI
>
> What the hell am I looking at!? Are you like... some kind of creature? ...A vampire or something?

> SILAS
>
> Yes... I'd prefer to just be called a vampire... I mean you no harm...

> TERI
>
> Oh my Lord! Are you serious!?

Teri stares at Silas' wings...

> SILAS
>
> My Lord as well ma'am... You can trust me... You don't need the bat... Would you like to sit down?

> TERI
>
> Right... Okay... A vampire is at my front door wanting to have a chat on my porch... Excuse me... I'm kinda freaked out right now...

Silas walks over to a wooden table on the porch.

                SILAS

Don't worry, I wont bite. I don't feed on humans.

Teri walks outside and cautiously walks to the table while still holding the bat...

Silas sits...

                SILAS

Do you need time to process everything?

                TERI

Um... well no... I wanna know what you want...

Teri cautiously sits...

                SILAS

I know all about you Teri... I know you and your late husband, tried to conceive...

                TERI

Wow... Okay right to this kind of stuff. Yeah we tried... a lot...

                SILAS

Sorry to be straight to the point.

                TERI

It's fine... How... how do you know... anything... about me?

                SILAS

I was led here by a holy vision... I'm here because I know a scientist that will help you conceive... but he will be using giant DNA.

TERI

Like... really big DNA?

SILAS

No, no... Are you familiar with The Nephilim?

TERI

Yeah... You mean, like... in The Bible right?

SILAS

Yes.

TERI

Oh... okay... Isn't that dangerous though?

SILAS

I assure you it wont be. They are just manipulating the DNA... Their growth wont really be too abnormal during your pregnancy... They will just carry the blood...

TERI

That sounds nuts... Me, giving birth to a giant?...

SILAS

Well actually... it doesn't have to be just one child... Anyway, they would only be half giant, just to be clear. I know you don't want to be alone, but it's up to you if you want to do this. You don't have to.

TERI

I'm already over 40... shouldn't you find someone else?...

>   SILAS
>   I was guided to YOU. You will be blessed... The
>   scientist will also make sure there are assisted
>   reproductive treatments...

>   TERI
>   I DO want children but this is crazy...

>   SILAS
>   I know. Take some time to think... I'll come
>   back.

Teri pauses...

Silas walks of the deck and flies off...

Teri looks at the ground for a moment...

INT. CAR - DAY

SUPER: TWENTY YEARS LATER

A women, Cheryl, 35, drives, and her son, David, 9, sits passenger.

They drive in a suburban area...

Cheryl makes a turn looking very confused...

After a moment she grabs her phone.

>   CHERYL
>   Man this stupid thing is so slow... Oh no...
>   damn... it died.

She sets the phone down...

>   DAVID
>   It's okay just make a left up here. It's about a
>   mile away...

Cheryl looks at David shocked...

>   CHERYL
>   What?

>   DAVID
>   I remember how to get there...

INT. CARL'S HOUSE - LIVING ROOM - DAY

The TV is on quietly in the middle of the room.

ON TV

The news plays a motorcycle chase...

The headline reads "LOCAL POLICE CHASE."

The living room has a coffee table, a couch, and a recliner...

Cheryl sits on the couch with David, and stirs a cup of tea.

Carl, 40, walks out with two sodas and hands one to David.

David opens it while watching the motorcycle chase on TV.

>   CHERYL
>   My phone was acting up, and David
>   remembered how to get here...

>   CARL
>   Really? He was so little last time.

                    DAVID
          Mom look he's passing that same gas station we
          went to on the way here.

Carl looks at the TV.

                    CARL
          You know it's the same one buddy?

Cheryl sips tea as David shakes his leg watching the chase...

                    DAVID
          It's by that run down burger spot, near the big
          rotted tree I saw.

                    CHERYL
          You remember that? I wasn't paying much
          attention on the drive...

                    DAVID
          Really?... I could remember everything on the
          whole drive...

David looks back at the TV...

                    CARL
          You know... I got a friend that works for the
          state. He specializes in testing gifted children. I
          can give him a call...

Cheryl nods...

                    CHERYL
          Yeah... okay.

INT. OFFICE - DAY

The office is small with a few file cabinets.

A teacher, Fred, 50, sits at a desk, and David patiently sits across from him.

Fred picks up the book "The Great Gatsby", from his desk, and hands it to David, then grabs another from inside his desk.

                    FRED
          I'm gonna start reading this, and later give you
          a very detailed test... okay?

                    DAVID
          Sure.

Fred and David open the book up.

                    FRED
          Alright, Chapter 1... In my younger and more
          vulnerable years...

INT. EMPTY CLASSROOM - DAY

David sits at a desk and fills out questions on a test...

INT. OFFICE - DAY (LATER)

Fred looks over the test.

                    FRED
          Well... it looks like you scored perfect... You
          really pay attention to detail don't you?...

David smiles.

                DAVID

        Yeah... I mean... It's easy for me.

David pauses and Fred opens the book...

                FRED

        I wanna try something... Can you remember...
        page 51... lines 21 through 23, from memory?

                DAVID

        Sure... What part of the Middle West? I inquired
        casually... San Francisco... I see...

INT. CHERYL'S HOUSE - KITCHEN - DAY

The kitchen is small with vintage appliances...

Fred and Cheryl sit at the kitchen table... Sunlight from a window above
the sink shines on them...

                FRED

        He knew every word... It's remarkable...
        especially from a nine year old...

Cheryl nods.

                CHERYL

        So he has good memorization skills?

                FRED

        Well... that would imply he was intentionally
        memorizing it... I believe it's much more than
        that... I think, he's got a rare gift...

Fred pauses and Cheryl stares at him patiently...

FRED
It's called hyperthymesia... Simply explained,
hyperthymesia is the inability to forget...

EXT. TERI'S - CABIN - DAY

The sun is going down and is behind the trees...

Silas watches Eli, 18, and Ben, 19, wrestle in the yard.

Eli and Ben are both around 6'2, 200 pounds, and muscular.

Near them is a half-built small log cabin style shed.

Teri stands on the porch, that now has many plants all over.

She walks up to Silas and watches the boys wrestle.

TERI
Do they always have to train Silas?

SILAS
They wanted to...

TERI
Why?

SILAS
This time?... Just for fun...

Eli gets Ben in an arm bar on the floor and Ben yells.

Eli wraps around Ben with his legs around his neck.

Ben gets on his knees, flexes and starts to lift Eli up.

Ben punches Eli in the side and Eli lets go and falls.

                    ELI
        Hey come on! We aren't striking.

                    BEN
        You were breaking my arm!

Teri laughs...

Silas smiles...

                    SILAS
        What is it?...

                    TERI
                  (to Silas)
        Their arms don't break...

                    ELI
        Tap next time Ben!

                    SILAS
        Hey you guys come on... Do something else.

Eli nods...

                    ELI
        Alright...

Eli looks at Ben and Ben stretches, then nods.

EXT. FOREST AREA - NIGHT (LATER)

Ben and Eli each hold axes near a large tree.

SERIES OF SHOTS of Ben and Eli chopping down a tree.

Eli swings his axe at the tree and yanks it out quickly.

Ben thrusts his axe into the tree and backs up.

Eli turns and chops at the tree with full force.

Ben spins and smashes the axe in the tree...

EXT. CABIN - FRONT YARD - NIGHT

Eli and Ben put the final board on the roof of the shed...

After a moment they both start chopping up some wood...

They start a fire near the shed, and sit by it.

Silas walks up and sits a bit further away from the fire than Ben and Eli.

>ELI
>Careful Silas, watch out for embers...

>SILAS
>I'll be fine...

>BEN
>All those gifts, yet a book of matches can take
>you out...

Eli looks at Ben and shakes his head...

EXT. CABIN - FORREST AREA - NIGHT (LATER)

Ben and Eli sleep in the shed and Silas lays down awake watching the fire...

After a moment he closes his eyes...

QUICK FLASH

EXT. UNDERGROUND CHURCH - SIDE OF CHURCH - NIGHT

Silas stands near a large stone tomb with his hand on it...

INSIDE TOMB

Angela lies inside screaming and punching the tomb...

                                                              BACK TO:

EXT. CABIN - FRONT YARD - NIGHT

Silas' eyes spring open...

He takes a deep breath, and shakes his head.

He puts his hands over his face, and sits up for a moment...

QUICK FLASH

EXT. COLORFUL PORTAL - DAY

The angels, Louis, Fredrick, and Anthony fall in a vortex.

The swirls transition to light green, then they slowly turn dark green, and after a moment the swirls turn red...

Louis watches the other two angels get swallowed into the red swirls in front of him but the portal suddenly disappears and Louis finds himself falling from the clouds toward a grass field on Earth...

He tries to flap his wings as he spirals down...

He puts his hands in front of him and slams on the ground.

He stands slowly, dusts himself off, and looks around, as his wings turn to ash.

WHITE SCREEN

INT. APARTMENT - BEDROOM - DAY

SUPER: PRESENT DAY...

In the bedroom, a muscular man, Joseph, 30, sleeps...

He looks like a complete clone of Louis but with a bald head.

He suddenly wakes up, and looks at his shoulders where Louis' wings were before they turned to ash...

FRONT ROOM

The large front room is attached to the kitchen.

There is a living room and a small dining area in the corner.

The living room has one couch, and a TV.

Joseph heads to the kitchen toward the refrigerator...

He opens it and starts drinking a small orange juice box...

He pauses... shakes his head, and exhales...

EXT. UNDERGROUND CHURCH - LARGE ROOM - NIGHT

Matthew, and Mammon walk into a dark room...

Matthew holds a man, Henry, 35, over his shoulder.

Henry wears a denim jacket and leather pants...

Mammon lights up the room with two fireballs...

MATTHEW
Who are you?...

Handcuffed to the concrete floor are a few skeletons...

Matthew drops Henry, and Henry stands and backs into a wall.

MAMMON
I can smell it inside you...

HENRY
What are you talking about?

MAMMON
Listen demon... I know your God cast you down
to hell... and you escaped to Earth...

Mammon grabs Henry and lifts him up by his shoulder...

HENRY
Nobody has EVER joined you two...

MAMMON
Oh, so you DO know of us?...

HENRY
You will never get any of us to swear allegiance
to you. We denounced God, then the Devil...
Why would any of us join you?

MATTHEW
Don't you realize Mammon can help you fully
transfer into this body!

HENRY

I... I won't be ruled...

MATTHEW

You are all raging and going berserk out there... it's pitiful. You need a leader... a master. It would benefit you to join us.

Henry pauses...

MAMMON

I'm done playing around with you demons! Now hear me when I say, you will be locked here until your body completely deteriorates like the others you see here... No food, no water... nothing. I know your demonic soul will keep a human body from rotting.

MATTHEW

One of you lived over a year...

MAMMON

You'll stay alive until your skin rots off and you turn to bones... We'll see if you still want to be stubborn once that happens.

Henry's eyes turn black and he starts growling and squirming.

He wiggles out of Mammon's grip...

Matthew tackles him and straps him to handcuffs bolted on the ground.

They back away and Henry starts to yell a high pitch screech.

Mammon and Matthew hear a loud slam from above...

EXT. UNDERGROUND CHURCH - SIDE OF CHURCH - NIGHT

Silas lands in the cave near the church...

He walks up to Angela's tomb on the side of the church...

Suddenly out of nowhere Mammon jumps and lands near Silas.

He punches Silas, and Silas goes flying...

He slams against the inner side of the cave and groans...

Mammon jumps over to Silas as he recovers...

He starts to create a fireball in his hands...

Matthew leaps nearly fifteen feet over to Mammon...

He looks at Mammon, and shakes his head.

Mammon absorbs the fireball back into his hand...

> MAMMON
> He was near the tomb. Tell me again why we
> didn't kill him before?...

> MATTHEW
> We didn't need to kill him... and we still don't
> need to. Silas, were you thinking of letting
> her out?

> SILAS
> I just wanted to visit...

> MATTHEW
> You never wanted to visit me.

Silas watches Mammon tighten his fists...

He quickly jumps and tries to fly off.

Mammon leaps up, grabs Silas, and slams him on the ground...

Matthew walks over to Silas as he starts to get up.

> MATTHEW
> She is too dangerous to let free... for everyone...
> You know that.

> MAMMON
> He wouldn't dare. Leave... weak vampire.

Mammon walks away and Matthew looks at Silas...

Silas jumps, and flies off.

> MATTHEW
> I can't always stop Mammon! You'll be on your
> own next time!...

> SILAS
> (to self)
> No I wont...

EXT. APARTMENT BUILDING - ROOFTOP - NIGHT

Joseph stands on the roof looking down at an alley below.

Across the street of the one-way alley, there are two dumpsters filled with trash.

Joseph takes a few steps back and exhales... He squeezes his hands together, and runs toward the edge...

He jumps, and falls straight toward the ground.

ALLEY

A police officer turns into the alley...

Joseph slams into one of the trash cans...

He gets out of the trash and dusts off...

The officer gets out of the car and runs up to Joseph...

> OFFICER
> You okay man? I heard that slam.

Joseph stretches.

> JOSEPH
> Yeah... I'm okay.

> OFFICER
> You just flew into that can!

> JOSEPH
> No I didn't... I just fell... I didn't fly...

> OFFICER
> Are you okay? Anything broken?

> JOSEPH
> I'm fine. Nothing is broken...

Joseph walks away...

> OFFICER
> Wait, let me get you to a hospital.

                    JOSEPH
        I just slipped. It's okay. Luckily I landed perfectly
        in the dumpster.

INT. TERI'S CABIN - KITCHEN

It is early morning and the kitchen is lit by outdoor light.

Silas walks up to the sink and splashes water in his face.

On the refrigerator is a magnet picture frame that says "IN MEMORY
OF" and there is a picture of Teri.

ON PICTURE

Teri, looks ill, but smiles, while standing in the middle of Ben and Eli,
who are now fully grown men...

After a moment Silas grabs a paper towel and dries off.

He closes his eyes tight, pauses and has quick visions...

SERIES OF FLASHES

Joseph tosses and turns in bed.

Louis flies through a portal.

Louis thrusts his claws into Silas's stomach.

Joseph wakes up on his bed panting...

SEQUENCE ENDS

Silas finishes drying his face...

EXT. TERI'S CABIN - DAY

The sun is still behind the hills.

Silas walks out onto the porch and squeezes his eyes shut.

He rubs his head for a moment and takes a deep breath...

He starts to have a vision...

QUICK FLASH

INT. JIM LETI'S MANSION - OFFICE - DAY

David, now 24 sits on one side of a desk...

David wears a collard shirt, and has a thin, cut build.

Across David, another man, Lawrence, 65, sits.

Lawrence wears a white button up T-shirt.

> LAWRENCE
> So let me explain everything... See this is a government funded program, originally ran by my mentor, Jim Leti, many years ago, before he left me everything. Today the government has practically no involvement in the process... Thankfully, they still have us in their budget though...

David leans forward in his chair.

> DAVID
> How is that?

LAWRENCE

They were really interested in this at the start, and that flame hasn't burnt out yet... We send progress reports, and they send checks.

DAVID

So, I read about it a little before I came, but tell me more about this program...

QUICK FLASH

INT. LAB - DAY

SUPER: 1984

Jim Leti, stands at a table wearing a lab coat looking at diagrams, neurology textbooks, and X-rays of the human brain.

A young man wearing gym clothes, Tommy, 20, runs on a treadmill in a room with large windows, next to the lab.

LAWRENCE'S VOICE

The original plan, was to find out just how hard we could push the human brain...

Jim walks over and watches Tommy run for a moment...

EXT. JIM'S MANSION - BACKYARD - LONG JUMP SETUP - DAY

A young man, Derek 25, wears a black muscle shirt tucked into short running shorts.

Derek stands at the starting point of the long jump.

Jim stands holding a clipboard, and smoking a cigarette.

The young man runs, and jumps...

> LAWRENCE'S VOICE
> The tests have always been designed to find each
> subject's limit...

Lawrence stands across the yard and watches Derek clear twenty-nine feet.

BACK TO:

INT. LAWRENCE'S MANSION - OFFICE - DAY

> LAWRENCE
> Some actually did break Olympic World
> Records... and almost all of the subject's I.Q.'s
> raised after all the assessments, and studying
> they did... but we never have reached the level
> of progress we thought we would. We hope we
> can reach that level with you. You are our first
> candidate to have hyperthymesia... Do you
> know what our original hypothesis was David?

> DAVID
> Yes... you set out to snap the subject's brain into
> overdrive...

Lawrence nods.

> LAWRENCE
> Yes... That was, and IS the goal...
> We may be able to show you how to do that...
> to put yourself on autopilot...

FLASH

EXT. TERI'S CABIN - FRONT PORCH - DAY

Silas' vision of David ends...

After a moment he hears leaves crunch in the woods...

He walks onto the yard, leaps and flies off...

EXT. WOODS - DAY

Silas lands near a cave that has a tall thin opening, with rocks on the sides that have plants growing over them...

He walks into the cave, turns around, and peeks out...

He notices a deer stop and eat some berries on the ground.

Silas starts to creep out slowly and steps on a branch...

The deer hears the crunch and runs off...

SILAS

Dammit...

Silas looks at the sky...

The sun is still behind the trees...

He closes his eyes and has another vision of David...

FLASHBACK SEQUENCE

EXT. MANSION - BACKYARD - DAY

A man holding a clipboard, Dan, 50, blows a whistle.

David runs a 100 yard hurtle track, set up in the backyard.

He perfectly hops over every hurtle, then turns around and runs back perfectly...

He runs up to Dan, as Dan stops his stopwatch.

> DAVID
> How did I do?

> DAN
> Better than last time as always...

David pulls a small hand towel out of his pocket...

INT. LAWRENCE'S MANSION - OFFICE

Lawrence sits behind his desk typing on a computer...

David walks in, wiping down sweat with a hand towel.

> LAWRENCE
> You're done for the day?

> DAVID
> Yeah... Hey, out of everything, as of right now,
> what am I best at?

David sits.

Lawrence types some more... then pauses and looks at his computer...

> LAWRENCE
> It's not what you'd expect.

                    DAVID
I'm just curious...

                    LAWRENCE
Diving...

                    DAVID
Really? Diving?... Cool...

                    LAWRENCE
Why do you think you're doing so good in that?

                    DAVID
I just feel like I'm concentrating without trying.
Like... I'm free.

FLASH

INT. INDOOR OLYMPIC SIZE SWIMMING POOL - DAY

David stands on the ten meter diving board facing backwards.

                    DAVID'S VOICE
        I feel anxious... but I can feel the calmness in
        the atmosphere... and I just try focus on that...

He jumps off, spins one and a half times, then somersaults two and a
half times and dives.

                                        BACK TO:

INT. LAWRENCE'S MANSION - OFFICE - DAY

                    LAWRENCE
That's interesting David...

                              DAVID
                    What about my fighting skills?

Lawrence folds his hands and puts his elbows on his desk.

                            LAWRENCE
                    Look, I know it's fun... but that training has
                    just as much relevance as any other physical or
                    mental training we do here.

                              DAVID
                    I understand... but I still wanna know... If that's
                    okay...

Lawrence smirks, nods, and looks at the computer.

QUICK FLASH

INT. INDOOR DOJO - DAY

David practices with an instructor, Tony, 40...

Tony holds patted gloves as David kicks his hands.

David high kicks with his left foot twice in a row, low kicks once with
his right, side kicks with his left, high kicks with his right, and spinning
back kicks with his left.

Tony briefly loses his balance.

                              TONY
                    Again!

                                                      BACK TO:

INT. LAWRENCE'S MANSION - OFFICE - DAY

DAVID
Am I doing any good in Boxing?

LAWRENCE
Looks like out of the fight training you are best
at Tae Kwon Do, actually... Kicking rather than
punching... Boxing is tough to master.

David nods his head.

SEQUENCE ENDS

BACK TO:

EXT. WOODS - CAVE - DAY

Silas' vision ends...

He opens his eyes and watches another deer for a moment...

The deer stops.

Silas zooms over and grabs it.

The deer tries to squirm but Silas bites it in the neck...

The deer stays calm for a moment... then Silas lets it go and it runs off...

Silas wipes his mouth and walks back into the cave...

INT. UNDERGROUND CHURCH - LARGE BASEMENT
AREA - NIGHT

Mammon, Matthew and Henry walk in the room.

Five women and eight men lie, chained to the floor.

Their clothes have deteriorated, and they are very skinny.

                    MAMMON
          You've all had time to think... Has anyone come
          to their senses?

Matthew looks around and notices a woman, Dana, 30, trying to raise
her hand...

                    DANA
          Yes... Me...

Mammon walks over and kneels near Dana...

                    MAMMON
          What is your name?

                    DANA
          Dana!

                    MAMMON
          Do you swear to join us?...

                    DANA
          Yes!

Henry walks over to Dana and kneels near her...

                    HENRY
          You're making the right choice...
          No need to be alone...

Matthew nods at Henry and he backs away...

Mammon puts his hand on her head and her head jerks, and whips for
a second before she sits completely frozen...

Her eyes turn black and she shakes her head for a moment.

A man near her, Marin, 40, looks at her...

Matthew unlocks Dana's chains and she stands...

Marin starts wiggling his hands... his fingernails are dirty, long, and sharp...

> MARIN
> Hey... Wait... I'm ready too...

INT. LAWRENCE'S MANSION - KITCHEN - NIGHT

David and Silas sit at the kitchen table, next to a window with the blinds closed...

The wall oven is now modern with a digital clock...

> SILAS
> Matthew is getting followers... demons. After many years of them resisting... His numbers are slowly growing... and he WILL get more...

> DAVID
> You said the future isn't set... How do you know they'll get more?

> SILAS
> They finally got one to join... and that one, helped convince more. It only makes sense the numbers will keep growing... I don't know what they will do with all that power.

> DAVID
> How exactly do your visions work?

> SILAS
>
> Well... I can't see everything... I'm gifted with cognition... It is strange... It's almost like an instinct, but if I don't focus I can miss it... I see the present, or something relevant from the past. It helps me decide my future.

QUICK FLASH

EXT. JUNGLE - NIGHT

A man, Soldier #1 20, runs through with a medic, Medic Man 21.

Soldier #1 and Medic Man run up to a wounded man, Wounded Man #1 19...

Medic Man crouches down, and pulls out his first aid kit...

Soldier #1 starts providing cover fire...

> SILAS' VOICE
>
> It's like being a medic on a battlefield... you can know what to do if you focus... and if you know what to do, you have to act...

BACK TO:

INT. LAWRENCE'S MANSION - KITCHEN - NIGHT

> DAVID
>
> So if the future isn't set... I am totally in control of deciding whether or not to come with you?

SILAS

Of course, but I have a good reason to think you will. I experienced your trials... I know your drive... I don't see why you wouldn't...

DAVID

Honestly... I can feel something telling me to go but, I don't know.

SILAS

Not knowing is a part of life, but knowing, is the very essence of life. It's your choice. We'd be better off with you though...

Lawrence walks into the room and looks at Silas...

LAWRENCE

David... What the hell is going on?

David exhales, looks at Silas, and raises his eyebrows.

DAVID
(to Silas)
Go ahead.

Silas takes off his trench coat, lifts his wings up and walks toward Lawrence...

SILAS

A scientist like yourself shouldn't be TOO surprised to find out a being like me exists.

LAWRENCE

I'm not actually...

SILAS

My name is Silas... Visions guided me here...
and believe it or not, they have guided me
here before. Many years ago I met with your
mentor... We talked in this very room... He
helped me clone two men that are still very
close to me...

Lawrence nods his head, and clears his throat...

LAWRENCE

I don't recall cloning experiments here...

Lawrence stares, and admires Silas' wings...

After a moment Silas walks over to the table and Lawrence follows...

DAVID

Obviously, Silas is a vampire... He's on a mission
to fight a group of demons and also another
vampire.

LAWRENCE

What? Demons?

DAVID

Yeah... He has two half-giants on his team right
now... Oh... and also there's an angel out there...

LAWRENCE

An angel?... What is happening?

SILAS

I'm here to ask for David's help defeating the
demons...

LAWRENCE
David... how... how do you feel about this?

DAVID
I don't know. What do you think?

LAWRENCE
You are your own person...

Lawrence looks toward the floor and sighs...

SILAS
(to Lawrence)
You don't think he's ready?...

Lawrence looks at David...

LAWRENCE
We can push more before you decide. It's up to you.

SILAS
We need to train together soon if we're going to fight Matthew and Mammon...

DAVID
I kind of feel that going is right.

SILAS
You see?... You're ready to do this...

David looks at Lawrence...

DAVID
I didn't say that... How could I know?... You don't know for sure if I'm ready either...

SILAS
You're right... I don't...

DAVID
What if we fail? A man of God like you would
say that you don't need to fear if you have faith...
but pulling this off isn't probable...

SILAS
I have faith... and I also have fear... I know we
can fail... but David... you know you'll be fine...

DAVID
I'm not sure I'll know what to do if I go with
you... One mistake, one bad choice... and I'm
dead...

SILAS
I've made bad choices... So I understand where
you're coming from.

DAVID
What do you mean?

SILAS
I've made some terrible mistakes in my, long
life...

Silas looks at the floor and for a moment there is silence.

DAVID
What terrible mistakes Silas?...
What did you do?

SILAS
Well... you mean besides the fact that I couldn't keep Matthew from the darkness?...

DAVID
That's not your mistake. He made a choice...

Silas pauses and looks toward the floor and sighs...

SILAS
I... cursed my own daughter...

David pauses...

FLASHBACK SEQUENCE

INT. UNDERGROUND CHURCH - MAIN HALL - NIGHT

Silas holds a closed bible and closes his eyes...

Other vampires sit around him...

Terrance stands at the altar reading the bible.

TERRANCE
The physical forces of evil that attack heavenly places...

White light comes from the cracks of Silas' closed eyes...

INT. SNOWY CABIN - DAY

The sun is behind the trees and hasn't risen...

Angela sits at a wooden desk brushing her hair, wearing a long nightgown.

Her mother, Kate, 40, walks into the room.

Angela continues to brush her hair.

Kate takes the brush from her and starts to brush her hair.

Angela smiles. After a moment she pauses and starts to cough.

Kate backs away.

Angela starts to twitch and falls on the floor.

> KATE
> Oh my God Angela!

Angela recovers for a moment, and grabs her mother.

> ANGELA
> Mother what's happening to me!

Angela lets out a loud growl.

Silas bursts into the room and kneels near Angela.

> KATE
> Silas! What are you doing here!? What have you
> become!?

Kate looks at Silas' fangs...

> SILAS
> I can't explain right now! She's turning!

> ANGELA
> Father!?

> SILAS
>
> Yes I'm here.

Angela growls again...

> ANGELA
>
> It hurts!

Silas picks her up.

> KATE
>
> What are you doing!?

> SILAS
>
> I may be able to help her.

Kate touches Silas' face...

> KATE
>
> What are you going to do to her!?

> SILAS
>
> I'm sorry I can't explain but I must go if I'm going to help her.

Silas runs out carrying Angela.

> SILAS' VOICE
>
> I turned her and we prayed asking for help, but all we got from The Lord... was a place to lock her in.

EXT. UNDERGROUND CAVE - SIDE OF CHURCH - NIGHT

On the side of the church a stone coffin appears from out of nowhere...

Silas kneels, praying beside the coffin.

Angela nervously stands behind Silas watching as the lid of the tomb lifts up by itself and slowly lands on the ground.

Silas stands and takes Angela's hand.

He hugs her, and she starts to cry.

> SILAS
> I am so sorry...

Angela suddenly grabs a small calvary saber from Silas' holster and tries to thrust it into her stomach...

Silas panics.

> SILAS
> Angela!

The sword fails to penetrate her skin... She growls and tries again and the sword breaks...

She drops to her knees and starts to cry... then after a moment she growls loudly, then catches her consciousness.

> ANGELA
> Oh no... you have to put me in there now! It's taking over!

Angela starts to twitch.

Silas holds her hand and walks her to the tomb...

They look at each other for a moment...

ANGELA
I'll wait for you to find a way to turn me back...

She lays down in the tomb...

Silas drops to his knees and prays.

The lid for the tomb rises up from the ground and covers her.

Tears fall from Silas' eyes and he touches the tomb...

BACK TO:

INT. LAWRENCE'S MANSION - KITCHEN - NIGHT

David looks at Silas and pauses.

SILAS
If I was focusing harder instead of panicking,
maybe I could have been shown exactly what
to do for her.

Her soul will always be trapped in her body because I turned her...

DAVID
I'm sorry to hear that Silas...

SILAS
Mistakes get made David... but you will be
cautious... You know your limit... I know things
can get messed up if we fight, but we must.

David pauses...

DAVID
Well Silas I still don't know...

Silas closes his eyes and has a vision...

He springs up.

QUICK FLASH

EXT. FORREST AREA - NIGHT

Three black SUV trucks speed through a dirt road.

BACK TO:

INT. LAWRENCE'S MANSION - KITCHEN - NIGHT

DAVID
What is it?

SILAS
I have to go! If your not ready, I can return in a
few days if you'd like...

DAVID
Let me sleep on it...

SILAS
Very well...

Silas nods, and walks out of the room.

INT. TERI'S CABIN - KITCHEN - NIGHT

Eli, now 6'7, sits at the table eating chicken and black beans with a
glass of tea.

The kitchen light is on, but in the dining room next to it, it is dark...

Flashes of siren lights light up the dining room.

Eli stands up and looks out of the window as three SUV trucks pull into the yard...

ELI

BEN!

Ben, now, 6'6, walks in energized.

ELI

Hey we got trouble.

Ben looks out of the window.

BEN

What the hell? Where is Silas?

ELI

Not sure...

EXT./INT. FRONT YARD - NIGHT

Four men in riot gear walk together toward the door holding a battering ram, while two trail behind them.

Ten other police men stay back near the vehicles holding shotguns.

The head cop, Taylor 40, stands in front of the other nine.

TAYLOR

Remember! Nobody use live rounds!

LIVING ROOM

Ben and Eli stare at the front door... They look at each other...

                            ELI
            That's a lot of men out there...

Ben smiles and nods...

                            BEN
            He said no live rounds. You think rubber
            bullets, or bean bags?

                            ELI
            Does it matter?

Ben smirks...

Ben and Eli stretch.

The men start hitting the door with the battering ram...

Ben opens the door and grabs the battering ram.

The cops look at Ben and Eli.

Everyone pauses...

Ben yanks the battering ram toward himself.

Cop#1, and Cop#2, fall forward.

The other two cops, Cop#3 and Cop#4, let go of the battering ram
when Ben yanks...

Ben walks out, drops the battering ram, and charges Cop#3.

Ben grabs him by the arm, pulls him closer and punches him in the face.

Cop#4 charges Ben.

Ben grabs Cop#4 by the waist and throws him across the porch into the hand railing.

Cop#1 and Cop#2 stand and rush Eli.

Cop#5, and Cop#6 charge Eli as well...

Eli punches Cop#1 in the face with a right hook, front kicks Cop #2, and punches Cop#5 in the gut.

He quickly backfists Cop#6 in the face and he slams on the ground.

Cop#5 leans down holding his gut, and Ben rushes over and punches him in the face, and he slams on the floor.

Ben and Eli run towards the other officers.

Ben runs towards an SUV to the right, and Eli goes left.

A bean bag hits Ben's gut, and he runs through it.

Eli runs toward an SUV, where two men, Officer#1 and Officer#2, stand behind the open doors, holding shotguns.

Three officers, Skinny Officer, Goggled Officer, and Mustache Officer are further back.

Eli jumps up on the SUV, rolls on top of it, and jumps off.

ON BEN

Ben rushes up to Taylor, yanks his shotgun from him, and hits him in the stomach with it.

ON ELI

Officer#1 and Officer#2 shoot Eli with bean bags.

Four bean bags smack Eli, and he stands still absorbing the damage...

Officer#1 aims at Eli, and Eli grabs Officer#1's shotgun out of his hands and hits him in the side with it...

Eli drops the shotgun and front kicks Officer #1.

Officer#1 slams against the SUV, denting it...

Officer#2 runs behind Eli, wraps his shotgun over his head and chokes him.

Goggled Officer runs up and shoots Eli in the gut with a bean bag.

Eli groans, and flips Officer#2 over his head, and slams him on top of Goggled Officer.

Eli looks at Officer#1, leans down and checks his pulse...

Skinny Officer runs up and shoots Eli with a bean bag.

Eli grabs the shotgun, and rips it out of Skinny Officer's hands and spin kicks him.

Skinny officer falls on the ground.

ON BEN

An officer, Officer#3, runs up and Ben throws the gun at him.

Officer#3 gets knocked out...

Three officers, Thin Officer, Big Head Officer, and Tone Officer, rush Ben.

Thin Officer shoots a bean bag at Ben.

Ben grabs Thin Officer's throat and slams him against the SUV.

He sweep kicks Tone Officer, grabs Big Head Officer by the waist and quickly hip tosses him.

ON ELI

Mustache Officer rushes up and shoots Eli in the back.

Eli turns, and bats the shotgun out of Mustache Officer's hands with the shotgun he's holding.

Ben runs up and headbutts Mustache Officer and he flies back.

Silas suddenly lands from the sky in front of the house, and a cloud of dirt flies up...

Eli throws the shotgun down.

Ben and Eli run over to Silas.

> BEN
> Silas what happened?

> SILAS
> Go get the truck. We need to go.

Ben runs over to the driveway and jumps in a pick up truck.

Silas looks around at all the knocked out men.

Eli huffs and puffs.

Ben pulls up in the truck and Silas and Eli hop in.

INT. BEN'S TRUCK - NIGHT

SILAS

Let's go. More will show up soon...

Ben looks at Eli as he struggles to catch his breath, and shakes his head.

BEN
(to Eli)
Catch your breath...

SILAS

Eli, you okay?

ELI

It hurt but I'm fine.

BEN

Well it felt great to let off that kind of aggression if you ask me...

ELI

It's different if you don't have much aggression...

SILAS

I can't believe I had no idea they were gonna do this...

BEN

No vision to warn you that some government organization is after us?

SILAS

No... not sure why... maybe I wasn't focusing hard enough... I only got a vision when they were on their way. A great number of things has been on my mind today.

ELI

It doesn't matter everyone is fine...

Eli calms down, takes a deep breath, and tries to breathe slower.

ELI

Man... They just came up guns blazing...

SILAS

They obviously weren't trying to kill us... They wanted to capture us...

BEN

Maybe to experiment on us?...

SILAS

I hope that's not the reason...

ELI

We're gonna have to find out.

SILAS

I agree and we will... however, I feel like they aren't really a threat we need to worry about just yet... There's a bigger threat right now.

ELI

What is it Silas?

SILAS

Matthew and Mammon are starting to get followers...

INT. LAWRENCE'S MANSION - STUDY ROOM - NIGHT

David sits on a couch near a computer desk reading.

Near the desk is a stack of books.

David finishes the book and sets it on the stack.

He gets up and walks over to the computer and sits down.

He moves the mouse causing the screen saver to go away, and a computer chess game comes on the screen.

He begins to play as black.

Lawrence walks by the study and notices David playing chess.

He watches David play for a minute...

He walks closer to David.

David pauses, and looks at Lawrence.

> LAWRENCE
> You said you would sleep on it.

> DAVID
> I can't sleep.

> LAWRENCE
> Playing chess wont help.

> DAVID
> Lawrence, do you know that after just two moves there are four hundred possibilities?

Lawrence nods...

LAWRENCE
Yes... and after eight there are two hundred and
eighty-eight billion...

ON COMPUTER SCREEN

The opponents king piece is cornered in H8, while David's queen piece
is on A8, and his rook piece is on E8.

DAVID
You have been stuffing so many things in my
head and I know so much now... and Silas comes
outta nowhere, and reminds me that there are
many things you can't know.

LAWRENCE
Of course there are...

DAVID
Like the future... Nobody can know the future...
but... that being said... I do believe I can help
Silas. I'm capable of it.

LAWRENCE
Are you sure you wanna go?

DAVID
No... but I'm gifted in some way... no matter how
you look at it... whether it be from assistance
from a higher power... or just a random snag in
my brain that knocked something loose...

LAWRENCE
Do you believe you have to go?

DAVID
No... but I believe I should...

INT. BEN'S TRUCK - NIGHT (LATER)

They drive in a forrest area...

BEN
So this angel you have to meet Silas... wouldn't
he pissed off that you killed him in his past life?

SILAS
I attacked him... but I didn't deliver any of the
fatal blows...

ELI
He's a human right now?

SILAS
Yes... but because of his soul, he may fully
become an angel...

BEN
He's just gonna come with us?

SILAS
He's an angel, and angels kill demons...

BEN
Why the hell are the demons taking up shelter
at the church?

SILAS
Matthew knows I swore to protect it when I
built it... We can't just use guns, explosives, or

fire on holy ground... They're using it because it protects the possessed while the numbers grow...

ELI

How are the demons allowed inside?

SILAS

Mammon is the only one that is in full demon form... HE can't step foot in the sanctuary... but with a possessed human, some of the spirit will always live on in the body, even if a demonic soul fully occupies it... So they can go in.

EXT. FORREST AREA - DAY

The sun is coming up...

After a moment Ben drives passed the trees, to a large open field.

On the field is a two-story house, and a barn...

A man, Gerald 55, with a thick muscular build, stands on his lawn feeding chickens.

EXT. GERALD'S HOUSE - FRONT YARD - DAY

Gerald looks up and notices the truck as it passes by some cattle behind a fence.

EXT. GERALD'S FARM - DIRT ROAD - DAY

Ben follows the dirt path to the barn, and parks inside.

INT. BARN - DAY

They all get out of the truck.

> SILAS

Right now, we need to train... you two aren't ready.

> ELI

We still train everyday Silas and you know why we slowed down...

> SILAS

Yes, and I miss your mother too... I wish she could be here giving us her love and support... but right now you guys gotta start training like before...

> BEN

We ARE trained Silas... Did you SEE what we just did?

> SILAS

You fought a bunch of average Joe's but you aren't ready for Mammon...

Gerald walks into the barn.

Eli walks up and shakes Gerald's hand.

> ELI

I'm Eli, this is my brother Ben.

> GERALD

Nice to meet you two.

Ben nods to Gerald.

> ELI

Thanks for letting us stay here.

                    GERALD

Of course. Anything for Silas... plus I got
some extra rooms.

                    SILAS

Hello Gerald...

                    GERALD

How have you been?

                    SILAS

Good... until recently...

                    GERALD

Let's get inside, we'll talk about it.

INT. GERALD'S HOUSE - KITCHEN - DAY

The four men walk in.

The kitchen is medium sized with a wooden table, and a three-part
counter top...

Gerald walks in and sits at his table, as does Silas.

Ben leans on a counter and looks toward Silas...

                    GERALD

What's going on... Everything gonna be okay
Silas?

                    SILAS

I'll explain in a moment, but everything
should be okay, as long as we succeed in our
mission. These two need to get outside and start
training...

                    BEN
What do you want us to do?

                    SILAS
Warm up. Practice whatever you want until
sundown... then I'll go out there with you...

                    BEN
I noticed some weights in the barn.

                    GERALD
Yeah, I just got a brand new bench.

INT. BARN - DAY

Eli lies on a weight bench gripping a straight bar, with seven, 45 pound
plates on both sides.

Eli lifts the bar up and lowers it to his chest.

                    BEN
Come on Eli! Up!

Eli lifts up the bar.

                    BEN
        One!

Eli lowers the bar again.

                    BEN
        Lift!

Eli lifts again.

BEN

Two!

EXT. GERALD'S FARM - YARD - DAY

Ben and Eli walk, each holding a large log, and they both set them down near the barn, where there are a few more logs.

INT. GERALD'S HOUSE - LIVING ROOM - DAY

The living room has a door to the yard, and two couches across from each other...

Dark curtains cover the windows.

Silas sits on a couch... After a moment he walks over to a window, and cautiously moves the curtain.

The sun is behind the trees...

EXT. GERALD'S HOUSE - FRONT PORCH - DAY

Silas walks passed a new half-built barn...

EXT. CREEK - SAME

Ben and Eli hold sticks, while standing on logs across from each other, trying to keep their balance.

They lock eyes.

Ben nods and after a moment Eli swings his stick at Ben.

Ben blocks and almost loses his balance, but recovers and swings at Eli.

Eli blocks and quickly returns another attack.

Ben blocks and the log rolls for a moment before Ben stops it.

Ben tries to swing but misses Eli because he is too far away.

Eli pokes Ben lightly, and Ben jumps, lands back on the log, and stands on one foot for a moment before falling.

Ben throws his stick at Eli as he falls into the water.

The stick hits Eli's fingers.

Eli groans, loses his balance, and falls into the water.

Silas stands in the woods watching them.

The two men walk out of the creek and up to Silas.

> ELI
> What's wrong with you man!?

> BEN
> Why did you push me?

> ELI
> Just take the loss!

> BEN
> Quit whining.

They approach Silas.

> ELI
> You didn't have to throw the stick.

Ben notices Silas.

> BEN
> Holy shit! I didn't see you there Silas.

> SILAS
> Working on balance?... That's good.

> BEN
> Yeah... and hand eye coordination.

Silas nods.

EXT. GERALD'S HOUSE - FRONT YARD - NIGHT

They stand away from the lawn in a dirt patch.

Ben stands blindfolded, holding two Y-shaped sticks.

Eli stands near Silas holding a long stick.

Silas sticks his hand out, and Eli hands him the stick.

> BEN
> Don't hit me too hard Silas.

> SILAS
> You can handle any attack from me.

Ben readies up.

> BEN
> Yeah but I don't want too... You can hit hard.

Silas grips the stick with two hands and approaches Ben.

                          SILAS
          I thought you get an adrenaline rush from being
          attacked.

                          BEN
          Not by you!

                          SILAS
          Mammon hits harder.

Silas swings at Ben, and Ben lifts his hands to block but raises them too
high and Silas hits him in the chest.

Ben groans, stops, listens to the steps, and to the wind...

Silas points the stick near Ben, then swings toward his arm.

Ben swings with his right knocking the stick away, and straightens his
stance...

Silas quickly swings at Ben, and Ben swats the stick away again...

Silas swings for Ben's gut and Ben blocks with both sticks.

Silas spins around, swings, and hits Ben in the back hard.

Ben tears off the blindfold.

                          BEN
          Silas what the hell!?

                          SILAS
          Your bones are solid as a rock Ben.

                          BEN
          Well your stronger than you think.

INT. LAWRENCE'S MANSION - BATHROOM - NIGHT (LATER)

David walks in the bathroom and starts brushing his teeth...

He pauses and looks out of his bathroom window.

Silas comes from the sky, onto the lawn.

EXT. LAWRENCE'S MANSION - FRONT YARD - NIGHT

Silas lands and starts walking toward the door...

INT. LAWRENCE'S MANSION - FRONT ROOM

The front room is large and open with a staircase.

David walks down the stairs and opens the front door.

                DAVID
        Come in.

Silas enters.

                SILAS
        So? Have you decided?

David nods...

                DAVID
        I'll go with you Silas.

                SILAS
        Are you sure?

David lightly laughs...

DAVID

As sure as I need to be...

SILAS

Thank you...

Lawrence stands at the top of the stairs.

LAWRENCE

I have a jet.

SILAS

Oh... Okay...

DAVID

You're gonna go Lawrence?

LAWRENCE

Of course.

EXT. CITY STREET - NIGHT

Matthew walks, down the street wearing a long coat, with two possessed men, Martin, 30, and Calvin, 27.

They walk behind a stumbling drunk man, Desta, 50.

Desta approaches an alley, and Martin and Calvin quickly run up and drag him into the alley...

Matthew checks the area for a moment, and walks toward Desta.

Martin and Calvin hold down Desta...

Matthew quickly bites Desta's neck...

INT. LAWRENCE'S PLANE - NIGHT

The plane has a small seating area with eight spaces...

Lawrence and Silas sit near each other behind a dinner stand, and David sits across from them...

> LAWRENCE
> As for this vampire Matthew... chop his damn head off, right?

Silas tilts his head.

> SILAS
> I don't think so. I've fought by his side. He is very overpowered. His skin may even be impenetrable.

David looks out of his window and stares at the moon as it peers through the clouds.

INT. UNDERGROUND CHURCH - BASEMENT - NIGHT

Eight possessed humans lie on the floor chained...

A crowd of two dozen possessed humans stand in the basement, looking at the chained up ones...

Matthew and Mammon walk in...

Matthew kneels near a chained woman, Tara, 35...

Mammon stands behind Matthew...

Tara's eyes turn black and the standing demons smile...

MAMMON
Are you ready to join us?...

Tara nods...

TARA
Yes...

Mammon... touches her head and she jerks her neck...

Matthew looks at Mammon... Mammon looks back and nods...

After a moment Tara slowly starts to move...

She stands and looks around the basement...

MATTHEW
Another one...

TARA
Silas is up to something... He has been training...

MATTHEW
Silas? What?...

TARA
I was told by the dark voices he's training with
a few skilled men...

MATTHEW
Dark voices?

MAMMON
You see Matthew! This is what happens when
you don't listen!

TARA
They have one more they will ask to join... one
very powerful man, but he doesn't yet know his
abilities.

MAMMON
Boris! Joshua! Andrea!

Three possessed humans, Boris 30, Joshua 25, and Andrea 28, begin to
approach Matthew and Mammon from the crowd...

Boris is thin and tall with long hair, Joshua is muscular with an eyebrow
piercing, and Andrea has long black hair, and tattoos on both wrists...

INT. GERALD'S HOUSE - LIVING ROOM - NIGHT

Eli walks into the living room from the kitchen...

Gerald sleeps on the couch sitting upright.

Ben sits on the other couch watching TV...

ON TV

A man leans on a table that has a spoon on the other side...

The spoon starts to bend...

BEN
No way... Is that real?

ELI
It's an illusion Ben.

BEN
I knew it...

Eli shakes his head...

> ELI
> Gerald, you gonna sleep out here?

Gerald wakes up.

> GERALD
> Oh thanks Eli.

Gerald gets up and walks out of the room...

Eli looks out of the window and sees Lawrence's jet...

He watches as it lands...

INT./EXT. LAWRENCE'S PLANE - SAME

Lawrence walks into the cockpit and talks to the pilot, Terry, 30

> LAWRENCE
> You can come inside with us?

> TERRY
> I'm fine hanging out in here.

> LAWRENCE
> There's a bed in the back, and food in the refrigerator.

> TERRY
> Okay thanks.

Silas, Lawrence, and David walk out of the plane.

Eli and Ben walk up and Eli shakes Lawrence's hand.

LAWRENCE
Nice to meet you I'm Lawrence.

ELI
Eli.

Eli shakes David's hand.

ELI
You must be David.

DAVID
Yeah... Nice to meet you.

David looks at Ben... Ben smiles and nods.

BEN
What now Silas? Get the angel?

SILAS
We can train with David for a bit.

ELI
So what can you do David?

DAVID
Well I've been training in-

LAWRENCE
Diving! He's best at diving.

BEN
Agile... good...

DAVID
Well yeah that... but also-

ELI
Let's build a diving board then!

EXT. FORREST AREA - NIGHT

Ben and Eli start chopping down a tree at a super fast pace.

They both hold axes with one hand.

David stands back holding an axe with both hands.

Ben hits the tree, and rips out the axe.

Wood chunks fly everywhere...

Eli twists and chops into the tree and yanks out the axe.

David runs up and swings the axe with both hands, then lets go of it with one hand and finishes the swing one handed.

Ben rushes up, turns and smashes his axe in the tree.

EXT. MOUNTAIN SIDE - ROAD - NIGHT

The possessed Boris, Joshua, and Andrea run down the road...

There is a parked car on the side of the road.

The three possessed slow down.

Boris looks at the other two, and they all rush to the car.

A man, Julian, 20, and a woman, Sophia, 20, kiss inside...

Boris breaks the driver's side window with his fist, unlocks the door and opens it.

He presses the unlock button, grabs Julian, and rips him out of the car.

Andrea grabs Sophia by her hair and yanks her out of the passenger seat.

> JULIAN
> Are you serious!?

Boris kicks Julian in the groin and Julian groans...

Joshua hops in the car and starts it.

Andrea gets in the passenger's seat, Boris jumps in the backseat and Joshua drives off.

EXT. LAKE AREA - NIGHT

Ben, Eli, and David carry logs toward a pile near the lake...

They walk up to the pile and drop the logs...

> BEN
> You getting tired?

> DAVID
> Not at all.

> ELI
> You were huffing and puffing.

> DAVID
> I'm good.

EXT. LAKE AREA - NIGHT (LATER)

Large outdoor lights attached to aluminum stands, shine, and light up a large area near the lake.

Lawrence and Silas sit on wooden chairs and watch Ben, Eli, and David build a 25 foot diving board.

Eli and David work on the ground, and secure one of the logs holding up the top platform, by burying it...

There are six large logs total standing upright.

There is one log on each corner, and two logs on the sides that have handles roughly carved in.

Ben climbs up one of the ladder logs and starts cranking down a bolt in a log...

David and Eli walk off.

EXT. FORREST AREA - NIGHT

Eli and David chop at a tree...

David swings his axe, two handed while swinging, but one handed at the final thrust...

Eli twists and smashes his axe deep into the tree...

EXT. LAKE AREA - NIGHT (LATER)

Ben, Eli, and David look at the finished diving board...

David wears a muscle shirt, swim shorts and aqua shoes...

He walks over to the ladder log and grabs on...

                              DAVID
                    Man... it's beautiful...

                    BEN
Wait... David what else do you do?

                    DAVID
I know some martial arts.

Silas and Lawrence stand...

                    BEN
Show us...

Lawrence and Silas start to walk over to the three men...

                    DAVID
Alright...

Lawrence and Silas approach the men...

                    SILAS
We don't have to see that just yet.

                    ELI
Yeah, let the man dive.

                    DAVID
It's fine.

                    LAWRENCE
David you don't gotta do this.

                    DAVID
It's better they see my potential.

                    SILAS
What do you want us to do David?

> DAVID
>
> How about you three try to hit me?...

> BEN
>
> Whoa whoa, I didn't say that.

> DAVID
>
> Come on. We need to train together right?

> SILAS
>
> Are you sure?

David nods, and stretches...

Silas gets close to Ben and Eli, and quietly speaks.

> SILAS
>
> Hey don't go full force...

> ELI
>
> Of course not.

> BEN
>
> Wait what?... I don't have a medium setting.

> ELI
>
> Just hold back a little.

> DAVID
>
> Hey you guys don't need to form a plan.

Silas, Ben and Eli stand across from David.

David cracks his knuckles, loosens up, and squeezes his hands into a fist...

The three men rush up to David.

Ben swings at David and he pulls his head back and dodges...

Eli swings immediately after and David twists out of the way.

Silas kicks at David's left side and David quickly blocks with his knee.

Ben kicks toward David and David blocks with the same knee that's raised.

Eli swings at David's right side and David drops to one knee and blocks with his forearm.

Ben swings at David, and David whips his neck back to dodge Ben's punch.

Eli quickly kicks toward David, and David drops to dodge the kick, and uses his hands to hold himself up.

Ben runs up and sweep kicks toward David and David pushes himself up with his hands and lands on his feet.

Silas swings at David, and David quickly twists and blocks with his arm...

David rolls back away from the three...

Ben runs up and swings at David, and David blocks with his left.

Eli swings and David blocks with his right, then David cartwheels away from them.

Silas kicks toward David and he quickly blocks with his leg.

Ben spin kicks toward David, and he twists out of the way.

Eli quickly swings and David pulls back just in time...

Silas swings at David's side and he spins dodging the punch.

David quickly ducks as Eli tries to hit him with a spin kick.

Eli swings at David, and he moves out of the way, then quickly twists to dodge a punch from Ben.

Ben swings at David's back and David whips forward, then Silas front kicks David and he blocks, but gets knocked back.

David twists and backs away and everyone pauses for a moment.

The three charge David...

Eli swings at David near his head, and David blocks. David then blocks a punch from Silas near his ribs, and quickly spins out of the way to avoid a punch from Ben.

Silas rushes toward David and swings forward and David jumps in the air over Silas, and does the splits above him.

David lands on his hands and rolls.

Ben rushes and swings at David and he blocks with both hands.

Eli does a spinning backfist, and David blocks and twists...

Ben swings at David's face and David shoots back and dodges.

David spins out of the way dodging a front kick from Silas.

Ben punches toward David and David blocks with his arm, then Eli runs up and front kicks, but David quickly backflips and Eli's kick hits Silas in the chest.

Silas goes flying and slams against a tree.

David pauses and looks at Silas.

Ben punches David in the face and David slams on the ground.

> LAWRENCE
> Hey, hey that's enough.

David quickly recovers and puts his fist up.

> BEN
> (to David)
> Shit... I didn't mean to do that man.

> DAVID
> I'm good, I'm good.

> ELI
> Are you sure?

> DAVID
> Yeah.

> ELI
> (to Ben)
> Good thing you were holding back.

> LAWRENCE
> All right that's it for now.

ON SILAS

Silas recovers then starts to rub his head.

QUICK FLASH

INT. JULIAN'S CAR - NIGHT

Joshua speeds on the freeway as the wind from the broken window blows Boris' and Andrea's hair...

                                         BACK TO:

EXT. LAKE AREA - NIGHT

Silas rubs his head.

Eli looks at Silas.

> ELI
>
> Shit...

Ben and David look over at Silas.

Eli and David start to run towards Silas...

> BEN
> (to Eli)
>
> Eli!...

Eli pauses.

> ELI
>
> What is it?

> BEN
>
> I didn't hold back on that punch...

Eli shakes his head...

> ELI
>
> Are you serious?... What the hell man?...

Eli runs over to Silas...

Lawrence runs up to David.

> LAWRENCE
> David are you okay?

> DAVID
> Yeah why?

> LAWRENCE
> He hit you hard...

> DAVID
> No, no I'm fine...

> LAWRENCE
> How?

> DAVID
> He must not have connected fully.

David runs to Silas...

> DAVID
> (to Silas)
> You okay?

> SILAS
> Yeah... but there's a different problem.

> ELI
> What?

> SILAS
> They're heading to Joseph's place.

                              DAVID
              The angel?

                              SILAS
              Yes.

INT. LAWRENCE'S PLANE - NIGHT

Ben, Eli, David, and Lawrence sit.

David now wears jeans and a T-shirt...

Silas talks to Terry in the cockpit.

                              SILAS
              That is the closest airport okay?

                              TERRY
              Yeah, got it.

Silas sits down.

                              SILAS
              Ben, Eli, you don't have to go.

                              ELI
              You said you don't feel like there will be a
              problem for a while...

                              SILAS
              I also thought we would stay at Gerald's...

                              BEN
              Who cares?... Let someone come after me and
              Eli again...

ELI

It's not like you to not know something.

SILAS

There's just a lot going on...

EXT. JOSEPH'S APARTMENT COMPLEX - OUTSIDE PARKING LOT - NIGHT

Joshua parks and the three possessed get out.

They run to a security gate and climb it quickly.

EXT. AIRPORT - NIGHT

Lawrence's plane lands on the strip and everyone gets out...

Silas types in Eli's phone and hands it to him.

SILAS

That's his address.

ELI

Got it.

Eli looks at Ben and Ben nods.

The brothers run off and climb a nearby fence.

SILAS

Okay David, I know it's kind of awkward.

DAVID

It's fine.

David kneels and sticks his hands up, and Silas grabs his hands, grips tight, leaps and starts flying...

They fly above Ben and Eli as they run very fast through a field near the airport.

ON GROUND

Ben and Eli hop another fence and reach a road.

A car passes and they cross and start running up the street on the sidewalk.

Eli, looks at his phone, notices some cars pass, hops over a parked car and crosses the street.

Ben follows Eli across the street and they run down a street in a nice neighborhood...

INT. JOSEPH'S APARTMENT - FRONT ROOM - NIGHT

There is loud knocking at the door...

Joseph walks up to the door wearing track pants, and a T-shirt.

He looks at the time on his microwave...

12:14 AM

He opens the door.

Boris, Andrea, and Joshua stand at the doorstep...

Their eyes turn black.

                    JOSEPH
              What the hell?

Joshua rushes to Joseph, grabs him by his shirt and throws him across the room into the kitchen, and Joseph slams into the refrigerator.

EXT. JOSEPH'S APARTMENT COMPLEX - INSIDE PARKING LOT - NIGHT

Silas lands with David...

Silas runs toward one of the apartment buildings and David follows.

Around the corner Ben and Eli hop a wall and rush toward Joseph's apartment.

INT. JOSEPH'S APARTMENT - KITCHEN - NIGHT

Joseph stands and coughs up some blood...

Boris runs over and punches Joseph in the stomach.

Boris raises his hand and swings again, and Joseph blocks.

Andrea kicks Joseph, and he slams against the wall.

Suddenly, Silas rushes into the apartment.

Joshua looks over and Silas pulls out his sword.

David runs in and Andrea and Boris run up to him.

Silas swings at Joshua and Joshua ducks, then Silas chops and Joshua spins out of the way.

Andrea and Boris approach David...

Andrea swings and David ducks and punches her in the ribs.

Boris swings at David and David blocks.

Suddenly Ben runs in and punches Boris in the head and he flies across the room, and slams into the wall...

Eli runs in, rushes up to Boris and knees him in the head.

Silas slashes Joshua in the chest...

Joshua steps closer to Silas and quickly kicks him in the stomach...

Silas drops to his knees...

Andrea swings at David's face and David dodges...

Eli runs up, grabs her, and throws her against the wall.

Joseph stands back in the corner and watches...

Andrea rushes Eli, jumps on his back, and starts pulling his hair and screaming.

Joshua looks at David and Ben, and rushes them...

David slides and trips Joshua and Ben punches Joshua in the chest.

Joshua slams against the wall and Silas runs up and chops his head off...

Eli grabs Andrea by the arm and slams her on the ground twice...

David looks around and closes the front door.

Joseph looks at Silas...

QUICK FLASH

EXT. OLD WOODEN CABIN - NIGHT

Silas and Louis press their swords together.

BACK TO:

INT. JOSEPH'S HOUSE - LIVING ROOM - NIGHT

> JOSEPH
> Who are you?

> SILAS
> I can explain everything but I'm sure they'll send more demons soon.

> JOSEPH
> They were demons?

> SILAS
> Yes... and you... are exactly what you think you are...

> JOSEPH
> What do you mean?

> SILAS
> You're an angel... This may seem odd, but I know about your dreams... I planned on coming here to ask you to come with us... but I waited too long and somehow, they found out how to get to you... Come with us... We can find your limit... Nobody is forcing you to though...

Joseph looks around his thrashed apartment...

INT. GERALD'S HOUSE - KITCHEN TABLE - NIGHT (LATER)

Ben and Eli sit at the table eating steak and brown rice.

Silas walks into the kitchen, gets a sealed bag of blood from the refrigerator and grabs a glass from the cupboard.

Ben stands and lifts his plate near Eli's.

> BEN
> Here you want it?

Eli nods while chewing.

Ben scrapes half of a steak and some rice off of his plate.

Silas pours the blood into the glass.

Ben walks over to the sink and washes off his plate.

> BEN
> Cow's blood?

Silas nods, and throws the plastic bag into a trash can under the sink.

> SILAS
> Would you like some?

> BEN
> No thanks... How is it compared to human blood?

> SILAS
> It's terrible... deer is a bit better...

LIVING ROOM

David sits on a couch with Lawrence...

Joseph sits across them looking nervous and tired.

DAVID
I know this all seems crazy... I just got here too...

Ben walks into the room.

DAVID
Hey I haven't slept much the past couple days...

BEN
Oh yeah. Gerald has a bunch of beds. Here let me show you...

David and Lawrence stand, and follow Ben upstairs...

Silas walks into the room and sits across from Joseph.

Eli walks through the room...

ELI
I'm gonna go to sleep too you guys... Nice to meet you Joseph.

JOSEPH
Thanks, you too man...

Eli walks into one of the rooms downstairs...

SILAS
Are you okay? Did they hurt you?

JOSEPH
I'm fine... So... my dreams... I remember... I attack you?

SILAS
Not really a dream...

          JOSEPH

A memory?

          SILAS

Yes... and your attacks were what made us turn into vampires in the first place. I've been alive ever since... Your soul is much different from a human soul, not to mention you were sent to serve in Hell, so when you died on Earth, you went to purgatory instead of Heaven or Hell. That is where you have been until this life...

          JOSEPH

What happened after my dream?... and how do you know all this?

Silas exhales and smirks...

EXT. GERALD'S HOUSE - FRONT YARD - NIGHT

Chickens walk around the yard gobbling...

INT. GERALD'S HOUSE - LIVING ROOM - NIGHT (LATER)

          JOSEPH

So that's it?... You need... my help, to stop this threat?...

          SILAS

Yes...

          JOSEPH

Are these possessed still human?

                    SILAS
In these demons, the soul is lost completely
from the men and women's bodies.

                    JOSEPH
Are there cases where the soul is still able to be
saved?...

Silas looks at the floor...

QUICK FLASH

EXT. UNDERGROUND CAVE - NIGHT

The tomb Angela is in rumbles...

INSIDE TOMB

Angela punches the stone tomb, screams and growls...

                                            BACK TO:

INT. GERALD'S HOUSE - LIVING ROOM - NIGHT

                    SILAS
Yes... and I'll let you know if we fight a possessed
person like that.

                    JOSEPH
How do we stop Matthew and Mammon?

                    SILAS
Our priority is to destroy the ones who joined
him... Matthew was given his power by God so
I wouldn't count on killing him for now...

                    JOSEPH
          It seems like we should try though.

                    SILAS
          Joseph, I do believe that with enough training
          you could harness the power to destroy
          Matthew... I believe we can all eventually be
          more powerful... but we don't have the time to
          train that hard now...

                    JOSEPH
          What about Mammon? Can we kill him?

QUICK FLASH

EXT. VOLCANO - OPENING ON TOP - NIGHT

Mammon stands near the volcano as lava bubbles behind him...

                    SILAS' VOICE
          He's one of the seven princes of Hell. He came
          to Earth long ago... precisely to team up with
          Matthew. He is extremely powerful.

After a moment Mammon squeezes his hands into a fist.

                                        BACK TO:

GERALD'S HOUSE - LIVING ROOM - NIGHT

                    SILAS
          I don't believe that killing him will be easy...
          The main goal is to interrupt their plans...

JOSEPH
Just because I have the soul of an angel doesn't
mean I can help.

SILAS
You will see in time... I can answer more
questions you may have later, but right now... I
need you to sprout those wings... We both know
they are dieing to come out.

JOSEPH
I don't know Silas...

SILAS
Yes you do. You tried before right?

JOSEPH
Yes...

SILAS
That time you knew you would land safely
in the trash cans... so of course they wouldn't
come out.

Joseph looks at the floor for a moment...

EXT. MOUNTAIN - CLIFF EDGE - NIGHT

Silas flies up to a cliff holding Joseph.

He lands, and lets go of him.

Joseph looks around, then at Silas.

SILAS
Whenever you're ready...

JOSEPH

I don't know...

SILAS

You have to believe you can...

Joseph walks up to the edge and looks down.

Silas walks up behind him.

SILAS

Close your eyes...

JOSEPH

Please don't push me.

SILAS

I wont...

Joseph closes his eyes.

SILAS

Imagine flying through the air. Visualize your
wings. That IS you... Believe it is you...

JOSEPH

Why am I up here? Why can't the wings appear
without me jumping.

SILAS

You have to fully believe you need them. Trust
they will sprout...

Joseph takes a deep breath, and jumps down...

He sticks his arms out.

His shoulder blades start to violently rumble...

Joseph yells as medium size, feathered wings rip out of his shoulders, and rip off his shirt.

Joseph can't catch himself with the wings and he nearly hits the ground, but a blue force field quickly surrounds him for a moment... then disappears, and he lands on the ground...

ON SILAS

                    SILAS
                   (to self)
              Wow... what is that?

ON JOSEPH

Joseph looks up at Silas, flies up to him and lands on the cliff...

                    JOSEPH
            I can't believe that worked...

                    SILAS
            Believe it... It's amazing.

Joseph looks at his wings, and nods...

                    JOSEPH
              It is...

                    SILAS
            How did you create that orb?

                    JOSEPH
              I have no idea...

SILAS

Let's hope you can use that later.

INT. GERALD'S HOUSE - LIVING ROOM - DAY

Joseph wakes up on the couch.

He rubs his eyes for a moment, stands up, and walks into the kitchen.

He walks over to the refrigerator, and pulls out eggs.

He grabs a pan hanging on the wall, puts it on the stove and starts cracking open some eggs.

LIVING ROOM (LATER)

Joseph sits eating the eggs, and watching TV.

Eli walks out into the living room wearing a black muscle shirt and sweat pants.

Eli rubs his eyes and looks at Joseph.

JOSEPH

How's it going?

ELI

What did I miss?

JOSEPH

Silas told me to jump off a cliff ...and I did...

EXT. GERALD'S HOUSE - FRONT YARD - DAY

Joseph, David, Ben, and Eli walk out of the house...

David wears swim clothes...

Joseph pulls his wings in close to his back, pops on a muscle shirt, and squeezes his wings through the shirt.

They pass the new, fully built barn, put up by Eli and Ben.

EXT. LAKE AREA - DAY

David stands on the diving board.

David jumps off and does four somersaults and one twist, before diving.

Joseph and Eli clap, and Ben smirks...

David walks out of the water.

> BEN
> Show off...

> ELI
> I will never be able to do that.

> JOSEPH
> Yeah that was nice David...

> DAVID
> Thanks.

Ben leans on one of the logs...

> BEN
> This thing could use more support.

> DAVID
> It seems okay.

                          BEN
              One or two more boards wont hurt...

Ben looks at Joseph, then at Eli, and Eli smirks and nods...

EXT. WOODS - DAY

Joseph, Ben and Eli each hold an axe, and take turns chopping,
powerfully and rapidly, at a tree.

Joseph, runs up and hits the tree, then yanks his axe out.

                          BEN
                       (to Joseph)
              You okay?

                        JOSEPH
              Yeah... Let's keep going...

They continue to take turns swinging at the tree as chunks of it fly
everywhere.

EXT. LAKE AREA - DAY

Joseph, David, and Eli watch Ben near the top of a ladder log, crank
down an additional log in the middle of the diving board.

EXT. GERALD'S HOUSE - FRONT YARD - NIGHT

Joseph, David, Ben, and Eli sit at a wooden picnic table.

                          BEN
              I want you to arm wrestle me.

Joseph nods.

> BEN
Focus... make whatever that's internal, become external.

Joseph nods his head again and takes a deep breath.

> ELI
You got this, alright?

Joseph nods, and locks arms with Ben.

> BEN
Ready?

> JOSEPH
Yeah.

They start...

David stares at the men's hands...

Ben tenses up.

Joseph remains calm and holds Ben back...

> ELI
Make your body work for you Joseph.

Joseph closes his eyes and stiffens his back.

Ben looks at Eli and smiles...

He starts to gain on Joseph for a moment...

Joseph starts to gain on Ben.

Ben exhales and starts to bring Joseph down.

Joseph groans, and his wings slowly lift up as he holds Ben back for a moment...

Ben slams down Joseph's hand.

Joseph looks down and exhales...

> ELI
> (to Joseph)
> Good job man.

Joseph stands.

> BEN
> Hey, this wasn't a pissing contest. I just want you to find your limit.

> JOSEPH
> Okay.

> BEN
> No hard feelings?

> JOSEPH
> Of course not.

> BEN
> Cool... I just don't want there to be any tension between us... Eli and Silas always complain about my attitude.

Joseph nods as he tries to catch his breath...

> ELI
> We don't complain.

BEN
Well you whine then...

Eli shakes his head.

Ben looks at Joseph.

BEN
We're good?

JOSEPH
Yeah man we're good.

Ben walks away...

ELI
Hey Joe... know that YOU are in control of your
body. It does what you want. Don't let your
body make YOU, do what IT, wants.

Joseph slowly takes a deep breath and nods.

INT. GERALD'S HOUSE - KITCHEN TABLE - NIGHT

On the stove there is a pot with pasta, a small pan with rice, a pot full
of veggies, and a pan with chicken.

Ben stands near the stove and flips a chicken wing...

Ben grabs a baking tray with potatoes out of the oven, with his bare
hands.

He grabs a plate from a cupboard, then grabs some veggies, chicken,
and salad from a large salad bowl on the counter...

He walks over and gives the plate to David...

David grabs some dressing and starts putting it on his salad.

Ben sets down a plate for Eli with everything on it.

Eli starts eating some grilled chicken and vegetables.

David starts eating as well...

Ben sets down a plate with everything but pasta, next to Joseph...

Ben stabs a chicken breast with a fork and sets it on a plate on the counter and starts eating while standing...

Joseph looks at the food.

Eli pauses as the food steams in his face.

David pauses for a moment, and looks at Joseph.

Joseph shuts his eyes and puts his hands together.

Eli pauses and looks at his food.

Eli bows his head, and stops chewing.

Ben sets down his fork, wipes his mouth, walks over and sets his hand on Joseph's shoulder and bows his head.

David bows his head and puts his hand on Eli's shoulder...

INT. GERALD'S HOUSE - LIVING ROOM - DAY

David, Silas, Joseph, Ben, and Eli stand in the living room.

Eli opens up a skinny shipping box and pulls out a staff wrapped in bubble wrap. On the bubble wrap is a large sticker that says "Graphene."

Ben opens up a box and unwraps brass knuckle knives.

Ben and Eli fold up the cardboard...

There are two more boxes next to each other...

David opens up a box with chrome metal gauntlets and Joseph opens a box with a Samurai sword...

David tries on the gauntlets and Joseph holds the sword...

> JOSEPH
> I don't know how to use a sword Silas...

> SILAS
> You did in your other life...

Joseph nods...

EXT. GERALD'S HOUSE - FRONT YARD - DAY

The sun is behind the trees and the farm is fully shaded.

Silas Gerald and Lawrence sit at a wooden outdoor table.

Ben and David train near the new barn.

They both stand in front of a punching bag setup that has had the bag replaced with a thick tree log.

Ben punches the log, and slices with both hands.

David, uppercuts, punches, and backfists the log.

Joseph and Eli practice near the picnic table.

Joseph holds his sword with the sheath on it, and Eli holds his staff with both hands.

Joseph grips his sword and charges.

Eli blocks, evades and sweeps at Joseph's feet.

Joseph jumps, and chops at Eli.

Eli blocks, rolls and swings at Joseph.

Joseph blocks, twists and swings at Eli.

Eli quickly blocks and the two take a few steps back.

They walk around each other cautiously...

> ELI
> You're doing great.

> JOSEPH
> Yeah I'm getting a lot better.

> ELI
> Your instincts are really good.

EXT. GERALD'S NEW BARN - NIGHT

The barn is mostly empty with two wooden tables...

Lawrence, David, and Ben, sit at one table, while Joseph and Eli sit on the other.

Silas stands in front of them all...

SILAS

Win or lose we need to know when to retreat...
If all we do is reduce the number of demons,
then that's still a major accomplishment...

BEN

We're not failing...

ELI

That's the spirit brother...

SILAS

We need to attack soon... Matthew has been
letting the demons wander about freely and
terrorize people... not to mention he somehow
was told where Joseph lives so he knows
about us...

ELI

We know Silas.

BEN

Will all the demons be at the church if they're
going out all the time?...

SILAS

We'll go Sunday... they can't harm people on
the sabbath... The three of you have trained with
each other a little... and that's very important
for team work. Now, it's time we go over the
plan. Mammon will be outside the church...
We will ALL take him on first, it doesn't matter
if we destroy him, or just incapacitate him,
but we can't go into the church if we can't get
past Mammon... While we are fighting him

Matthew will probably come out, and when he
does, Joseph and I will take him.

BEN
When you say take him?

SILAS
We've been over this...

BEN
If I'm near Matthew and I can go in for the kill
I'm doing it.

SILAS
How do you plan on doing that Ben? We don't
know Matthews limit... We don't really know
his power...

LAWRENCE
Silas, can't David try?

SILAS
To kill Matthew?

LAWRENCE
No... I just mean to, fight him... Hold him back
or... whatever...

DAVID
We should just follow Silas' plan.

LAWRENCE
If David fights Matthew, there is more of you
guys fighting Mammon.

SILAS
You wanna do this David?

Everyone looks at David.

DAVID
I think I can hold him off.

Silas smirks...

FLASH

INT. LARGE DARK ROOM - CAGE - NIGHT

David stands in a large cage with a lion.

They both stand facing each other...

David walks forward and the lion steps back...

After a moment the lion roars, and steps forward...

David freezes, and the lion does as well...

David sits and after a moment the lion also sits...

David listens as the lion breathes...

INT. GERALD'S HOUSE - BEDROOM - DAY

David quickly wakes up in a small room, laying on a bed...

He shakes his head and stands...

INT. GERALD'S HOUSE - BEDROOM - DAY

It is early morning...

Silas sleeps in a small bed in a mostly empty room...

QUICK FLASH

EXT. UNDERGROUND CAVE - NIGHT

The tomb Angela is in rumbles...

INSIDE TOMB

Angela punches the stone tomb, and yells...

BACK TO:

INT. GERALD'S HOUSE - BEDROOM - DAY

Silas wakes up and slowly runs his hands through his face...

EXT. GERALD'S HOUSE - FIELD - DAY

Joseph, David, Silas, Lawrence, Ben, and Eli walk toward the plane.

They all get inside and the door shuts...

Gerald stands on his lawn and watches as the plane takes off...

INT. LAWRENCE'S PLANE - DAY (LATER)

David sits near Ben, Joseph sits by Eli, and Lawrence sits near them by Silas...

Joseph and Eli bow their heads, and pray together.

David looks out the window at the clouds...

EXT. FORREST AREA - DAY

The sun hasn't risen, and it is still shady in the forrest.

The plane lands in an open patch.

Everyone exits the plane except for Lawrence and Terry.

David wears his gauntlets, Ben holds his knives, Eli's staff is strapped on his back, and Silas and Joseph both have their swords holstered on their belts.

Silas leads the way deeper into the forest, to the entrance of the tunnel that leads to the underground church.

They each hop in the hole in the ground...

Eli looks at the hollowed out rock forming the tunnel.

> SILAS
> This way.

Everyone follows Silas.

> ELI
> Silas, how could these tunnels have been made?
> This is solid rock...

Ben looks in the other direction of the tunnel.

> SILAS
> Your ancestors made them many years ago.
> They go all around the world.

> ELI
> Really?

Silas nods and they continue to walk...

> SILAS
> Is everybody ready?...

> BEN
> Come on everyone! This is it...

Ben grips his brass knuckle knives...

Joseph and Silas pull out their swords.

Eli punches his open hand and looks at David.

David smiles and squeezes his hands into fists...

They all turn the corner and walk into the large cave area...

Large hanging lanterns hang in front of the church...

There are two large windows in front, and the light from the lanterns lights up the inside of the church...

The Man, The Angel, The Vampire, and The Giants, all walk toward the church...

Mammon jumps off the top of the church and looks at everyone.

They all start to run and Mammon roars...

INT. UNDERGROUND CHURCH - MAIN HALL - NIGHT

Matthew sits leaning on a chair at the altar reading a large jet black book.

The possessed men and women, sit in the pews...

Some sit reading alone, and others sit in groups, talking...

They all hear the roar from Mammon and pause...

MATTHEW
EVERYONE STAY IN HERE!

EXT. UNDERGROUND CHURCH - NIGHT

Silas and the others start to run toward Mammon.

Ben rushes passed everyone, and gets to Mammon first.

Mammon stands still.

Ben smashes his fist into Mammon's chest.

Mammon groans, and gets slightly pushed back.

He throws a fireball at Ben's chest, and Ben flies back past everyone and drags across the ground...

Eli rushes up to Mammon and swings towards his head.

Mammon blocks with his forearm, and punches Eli with an uppercut to the stomach with his left, then hits him in the face with a right punch that knocks him down.

Ben recovers.

Joseph flies and smashes his shoulder into Mammon's head.

Mammon grabs Joseph by his wing as he tries to fly away.

David runs up Mammon's chest, backflips and kicks him in the face.

Joseph starts to rip away from Mammon's grip and yells...

Silas rushes up and thrusts his sword into Mammon's chin and lava-like blood drips down...

The wound starts healing immediately.

Joseph gets free and flies off.

Silas pulls the sword out and Mammon swats Silas with the back of his hand, and Silas goes flying...

Ben runs up and uppercuts Mammon in the face.

Mammon swings at Ben and Joseph flies up and blocks his fist with his sword.

David runs up Joseph's back and spin kicks Mammon...

Ben hits Mammon in the ribs, and slices.

Mammon grabs Joseph by his wing, and slams him on the ground.

David runs over to Joseph and helps him up.

                    DAVID
          Sorry man I saw an opportunity.

                    JOSEPH
              Na, it's fine...

Mammon punches Ben in the face and Ben slams down.

Ben recovers quickly.

Eli runs up and front kicks Mammon in his side.

Mammon groans, grabs Eli's leg, and throws him.

Silas runs up and sees an opening to stab Mammon's heart.

Mammon turns to Silas, and punches him, and Silas slams on the ground...

Eli gets up and runs toward Mammon, and Mammon quickly hurls a fireball at him, and Eli gets hit and falls down...

Matthew comes out of the front of the church with a sword...

Silas stands, and looks at David.

David nods, and rushes up to Matthew.

Mammon pauses, and roars...

> MATTHEW
> Silas what are you doing here!?

> SILAS
> You knew this day would come!

> MATTHEW
> (to David)
> Who are you!?

> DAVID
> I'm trying to figure that out...

David swings a right hook at Matthew.

Matthew blocks with his sword, twists and swings.

David ducks and swings again at Matthew and he blocks.

ON MAMMON

Ben and Eli rush up and Ben punches Mammon in his side.

Mammon grabs Ben by the throat.

Silas rushes up, twists and slices Mammon's arm.

Mammon lets go of Ben...

Eli runs up and punches Mammon in the ribs with an uppercut.

ON DAVID

Matthew slices toward David's face.

David leans away, and watches the sword pass his eye...

David turns, grabs Matthew from behind and squeezes his gauntlets around Matthews neck.

Matthew yells, elbows David in the ribs and rips away...

They start to move faster and faster...

Matthew quickly swings his sword at David.

David ducks and spin kicks toward Matthew.

Matthew evades and David crouches, and sweeps at his feet.

Matthew back flips, lands, and chops at David.

David quickly blocks with his right gauntlet.

ON MAMMON

Mammon kicks Eli in the stomach, knocking him back slightly.

Joseph flies towards Mammon, flips and launches his sword into Mammon's eye.

Mammon roars, pulls the sword out and throws it away...

INT. UNDERGROUND CHURCH - FRONT ROOM - NIGHT

Several possessed men and women stand near the front door...

EXT. UNDERGROUND CHURCH - FRONT AREA - NIGHT

Joseph runs over and grabs his sword...

Silas slashes at Mammon's chest.

Mammon spins and kicks Silas in the chest and Silas slams on the ground, Silas quickly rolls over and stands.

Ben elbows Mammon in the chest with his right, and punches Mammon in the stomach with his left, slicing down with both hits.

Mammon punches Ben in his face and he slams on the ground.

Silas runs up, spins and slices Mammon's right leg.

Mammon grabs Silas by the head and lifts him up.

Joseph runs up and stabs Mammon in his back and Mammon gets pushed forward but still holds onto Silas...

Mammon turns around and backhands Joseph away.

Ben lies flat on the ground...

Silas looks into Mammon's eyes... then looks over at Angela's tomb and stares for a moment...

Mammon slams Silas on the ground...

ON DAVID

Matthew swings his sword at David's head, and David ducks.

He then chops towards David, and David quickly blocks.

Matthew swings again, and David grabs his sword.

Matthew freezes, and tries to rip it away from David.

David yanks the sword away and tosses it.

Matthew punches David with a right hook...

David grabs his mouth.

ON BEN

Ben stands and looks over at David holding his jaw...

ON DAVID

Matthew punches David again in the face and David falls to his hands and knees...

Matthew looks at David angrily and David smiles...

> DAVID
> You're not that tough.

David stands.

ON MAMMON

Ben nods his head to Eli.

Ben and Eli run up to Mammon...

Eli swings a right hook at Mammon and he blocks.

Ben punches Mammon twice in the stomach.

Mammon puts his hands together, hammers down on Ben's head, and backfists Eli away.

ON SILAS

Joseph rushes over to Silas.

> SILAS
> (to Joseph)
> We have to go the side of the church.

Joseph helps Silas up.

> JOSEPH
> What?

> SILAS
> We can't beat him... Come on...

Silas picks up his sword.

Joseph and Silas fly over to the side of the church.

Eli and Ben look at them fly away.

SIDE OF CHURCH

Silas and Joseph stand near the tomb.

> JOSEPH
> Silas we can't let her out?

SILAS

I believe we must... She'll fight us... but I might be able to perform mind control on her.

JOSEPH

You MIGHT be able to!?

SILAS

Her brain is constantly battling the demon in her. Her mental state is so engaged, mind control should work...

JOSEPH

Silas why didn't we plan this!?

SILAS

Mammon is much stronger than I anticipated...

ON MAMMON

Mammon swings at ELI.

Ben runs up and blocks the punch with both forearms.

Eli punches Mammon and Mammon blocks, so Eli hits him in the wrists repeatedly, and Mammon backs up...

Ben and Eli step back as well.

Mammon roars...

SIDE OF CHURCH

> SILAS
> She may be more powerful than Mammon... but
> we only need to hold her still for a moment... I
> should be able to control her after that...

Silas kneels and starts praying...

> SILAS
> Come on...

Joseph kneels as well... and the lid of the tomb opens up.

Silas and Joseph stand and begin to back away some distance.

Angela stands up, wearing withered clothing.

Her body shows, and she has become much, stronger, and fit.

She roars...

ON MAMMON

Mammon, Eli and Ben look over at Angela for a moment...

Eli looks at Mammon, runs up and hits him twice in the ribs.

Mammon punches Eli, and Eli holds his stance.

Mammon swings at Ben, and Ben rolls out of the way.

ON DAVID

David and Matthew stop and look over at Angela...

After a moment David swings at Matthew with a right, then left, and
Matthew blocks both blows with his arms.

Matthew kicks toward David, and David blocks with his knee.

David spin kicks twice more at Matthew, and Matthew quickly blocks both kicks.

SIDE OF CHURCH

Joseph looks at Silas and Silas drops his sword...

> SILAS
> Your sword will be useless. You only need your
> hands to hold her.

Joseph drops his sword...

> SILAS
> Careful, she'll probably try to tear our heads off...

Angela jumps into the air and lands in front of Silas and Joseph.

She grabs Silas by the shoulder and head.

Silas drops to his knees.

Joseph quickly grabs her arms.

She lets go of Silas, and punches Joseph and he gets launched...

She grabs Silas' arm and tosses him.

Angela rushes up to Joseph and punches him in the chest.

Silas flies up, grabs her shoulders and yanks her down.

He stands above her and looks in her eyes.

Angela kicks Silas in the head from the ground and quickly stands up.

ON MAMMON

Ben and Eli rush up to Mammon.

Ben jumps and punches Mammon in the face and Mammon absorbs the punch.

Eli quickly hits Mammon in the stomach and Mammon gets slightly pushed back.

Mammon kicks Ben in the chest, then backhands Eli in the face and they both slam down.

SIDE OF CHURCH

Joseph tackles Angela and holds her tight.

She rolls over and starts punching Joseph repeatedly into the ground...

The ground rumbles.

ON DAVID

Matthew swings at David and David ducks, twists and swings a right hook at Matthew, and Matthew blocks.

Matthew kicks toward David, and David grabs his foot.

Matthew lunges back on one foot, and David falls to the floor.

David recovers, runs up to Matthew and spin kicks toward him.

Matthew blocks, and swings his fist at David.

David twists out of the way and kicks toward Matthew.

Matthew grabs his leg, and David, in mid air, twists his body and kicks Matthew in the neck.

Matthew gets knocked down.

Angela roars like a lion and David looks over at her...

Matthew quickly recovers.

David runs over to Joseph and Silas.

SIDE OF CHURCH

Angela continues to pummel Joseph.

Silas and David yank Angela away from Joseph.

Angela grabs Silas' arm, and breaks it.

David looks at Angela...

Angela stares at David and freezes...

David freezes as well.

Silas groans, and pops his arm in place, and it heals...

David looks into Angela's eyes...

Angela circles around David...

Joseph and Silas freeze, and watch them.

Joseph slowly creeps up, and quickly grabs her and puts her in a headlock.

Silas runs up and looks in her eyes.

Angela violently squirms and yells.

Silas waves his hand in her face and amber mist hits her...

JOSEPH
Do you have her!

SILAS
Yes!

Joseph turns around and sees Matthew leaping toward them with his sword in hand...

Angela takes a step forward, and punches Matthew in the face.

Matthew drops his sword and goes flying...

Matthew slams on the ground and drags on the dirt for a moment...

ON MAMMON

Ben swings at Mammon, and Mammon blocks.

Mammon hits Ben with a powerful punch that knocks him back...

SIDE OF CHURCH

Silas looks at Angela and they nod to each other...

She leaps toward Mammon...

Joseph stares at Matthew.

Silas looks at David...

                          SILAS
          Get Ben and Eli and go inside the church. She
          will fight Mammon... We'll hold off Matthew...

David runs toward Ben and Eli.

ON MAMMON

Mammon roars at Ben and Eli as they rush toward him.

Angela lands in front of Mammon in a kneeling stance, and slowly
rises...

Ben, Eli, and Mammon freeze.

Mammon rushes up to her and punches her...

She blocks, and does not budge...

Angela swings at Mammon, and Mammon blocks with both wrists,
and gets pushed back...

Ben and Eli look at Angela.

David runs up.

                          DAVID
          Come on... she'll take care of him. Silas has her
          under mind control.

Ben and Eli nod.

Angela continues to punch Mammon's wrists.

Mammon's defense breaks and she hits him in the face with a right
punch, a left, and another right.

Each punch she hits him with gets more powerful...

Mammon backs out of the way and runs toward the church.

Angela runs toward him and he turns around and throws two fireballs at her.

Angela gets knocked down from the fireballs, but quickly recovers...

She stands, and runs up behind Mammon, grabs him by the horns and yanks him to the ground...

She walks to the other side of him and kicks him in the

stomach and he slides further away from the entrance...

ON SILAS

Joseph and Silas get their swords as Matthew recovers.

FRONT OF CHURCH

David, Ben, and Eli run towards the church entrance.

INT. UNDERGROUND CHURCH - FRONT ROOM - NIGHT

The possessed angrily growl under their breath and their eyes turn black...

David, Eli and Ben enter the front room of the church.

Eli pulls the staff from his back.

In the front room there are stairwells on both sides filled with possessed humans.

Five possessed rush up...

David runs up, flips and twists over a few possessed, then backflips and kicks Possessed man #1 in the head causing him to flip, and slam on the floor.

All the possessed yell in anger.

Ben slashes Possessed Man#2 in the ribs and Possessed Woman #1 rushes Ben, and he quickly kicks her in her side.

Possessed Man #3 and Possessed Woman #2 rush Eli.

Eli runs up and hits Possessed Woman #2 in the stomach with his staff, turns, and smashes his staff into the head of Possessed Man #3, and he falls on the floor...

A possessed man, Possessed Man #4 rushes David.

David kicks Possessed man #4 in the stomach, holds his leg up as the possessed man falls, lifts it higher, and stomps on his stomach.

EXT. UNDERGROUND CHURCH - NIGHT

Angela runs up and uppercuts Mammon in the gut and he leans down.

She kicks him in the face, and he slams on the ground.

She jumps on him, grabs his horns and starts pulling.

Mammon groans, and Angela screams as she yanks the horns...

SIDE OF CHURCH

Matthew picks up his sword and Silas and Joseph approach him.

They stand on opposite sides of Matthew and he looks at both of them, and slowly turns full circle...

Matthew slashes at Joseph and Joseph deflects the blow.

He front kicks Joseph in the chest and Joseph flies back.

Matthew turns, chops at Silas, and Silas blocks.

Joseph gets up and swings his sword at Matthew and Matthew blocks.

Silas slashes at Matthew's mid-section, and Matthew jumps up and kicks Joseph and Silas in the face at the same time, and lands.

He quickly turns and chops at Silas.

Silas blocks and they press their swords against each other for a moment and Matthew turns and kicks Silas in the head.

INT. UNDERGROUND CHURCH - FRONT ROOM - SAME

David quickly runs up to another possessed, Possessed Woman #3, grabs her by the arm and slams her into a wall.

Ben rushes up to a possessed male, Possessed Man #5, stabs him in the gut with both knives, lifts him, and tosses him.

Two possessed, Possessed Man #6, and Possessed Woman #4, rush David.

David grabs Possessed Woman #4 by the hip, flips her, and tosses her on the ground.

Possessed Man #6 kicks toward David, and David blocks, and spin kicks him in head.

Two more possessed, Possessed Woman #5, and Possessed Man #7 run up to Eli.

Eli swings his staff at Possessed Woman #5, hits her in the back, and she falls...

He spins and swings upward, hitting Possessed Man #7 in the chin.

Four possessed men, Possessed Man #8, #9, #10, and #11, run up to David.

David grabs Possessed Man #8's arm, twists and punches him in the throat. He quickly twists, and spin kicks Possessed Man #9 in the head, then cartwheels and wraps his legs around Possessed man #10's neck, flips his body to the ground and punches him in the face.

Possessed Man #11 tightens his fists, and David launches himself from a kneeling stance, and knees Possessed Man #11 in the face.

EXT. UNDERGROUND CHURCH - NIGHT

Mammon grabs Angela and tosses her away.

She lands and Mammon creates fireballs in each hand and throws them both at Angela.

Angela stands, and blocks, but the fireballs knock her down.

Mammon rushes over to Angela and gets on top of her.

Mammon lifts up his right hand to hit Angela, and Angela grabs Mammon's arms, puts her foot on Mammon's stomach and flips him over her.

He slams down, and recovers quickly...

Angela stands, and back flips, kicking Mammon in the chin with both feet, one after the other.

Mammon launches back, and falls on his back...

Angela jumps on him again and repeatedly punches him.

INT. UNDERGROUND CHURCH - FRONT ROOM - SAME

Two possessed, Possessed Woman #6, and Possessed Male #12 rush Ben.

Ben turns and front kicks Possessed Male #12 and he flies back and knocks into Possessed Female #6 causing them both to fall.

They recover and run up to Ben again. He punches Possessed Male #12 in the face, and slices.

Possessed Female #6 runs up and punches Ben in the ribs, and Ben grabs her, picks her up, and slams her on the ground.

EXT. UNDERGROUND CHURCH - SIDE OF CHURCH - SAME

Silas recovers and rushes to Matthew, and Matthew turns and front kicks him in the chest.

Joseph swings down at Matthew and Matthew blocks and punches Joseph in the face with a hard right, and Joseph falls.

Matthew turns to Silas and stabs him in the chest, then kicks him with a spinning back kick, breaking his neck.

Joseph stands...

Silas slowly snaps his neck back into place...

Matthew breathes heavily and looks at Joseph and Silas...

EXT. UNDERGROUND CHURCH - FRONT ROOM - SAME

Three possessed, Possessed Man #13, Possessed Man #14 and Possessed Man #15, run up to David.

David spinning back kicks Possessed Man #13 in the chest and he flies into Possessed Man #14, squeezing him into a wall.

Possessed Man #13 hits the floor but Possessed Man #14 recovers and rushes David.

Possessed Man #15 swings at David, and David turns behind him, and wraps his arms around his head.

Possessed Man #14 approaches David from the back, and David jumps up and kicks Possessed Man #14 with both feet, slamming Possessed Man #15 down in the process.

EXT. UNDERGROUND CHURCH - SAME

Angela punches Mammon twice, then rushes to his head and starts to yank on his horns.

MAMMON
Get off me!

SIDE OF CHURCH

Silas stands and shrugs his shoulders.

Joseph runs up to Matthew and starts swinging his sword fiercely at him, with a left, right, then a forceful chop.

Matthew struggles to block the three attacks, but manages to bat Joseph's sword away with a jolt of energy.

Joseph pauses, and Matthew swings at Joseph and Joseph stops the blade with his hands...

Matthew panics and starts to press harder on Joseph's skin...

Joseph's hands drip a small amount of blood...

Matthew kicks Joseph in the chest, and hits him with a powerful punch and Joseph slams down...

Matthew starts to run toward the church...

Joseph spits blood and stands...

He flies toward Matthew, picks him up by the shoulders and throws him further away from the church...

INT. UNDERGROUND CHURCH - FRONT ROOM - SAME

Two male possessed Possessed Man #16, and Possessed Man #17 run up to Eli.

Eli hits them both in the head with his staff.

Possessed Man #16 falls on the floor and #17 stays standing.

Eli sweeps at Possessed Man #17's feet, tripping him, and stomps on his chest...

Marin rushes up to Eli from nowhere, and slashes Eli's back with his dirty sharp nails, and Eli turns around and smashes his staff into Marin's face...

One male, and one female possessed, Possessed Man #18, and Possessed Woman #7 rush David into a corner.

David leans on the wall, leaps up and kicks both possessed...

Three possessed males, Possessed Man #18, #19, and #20 run up to Ben.

Possessed Man #18 kicks Ben in his side, and Ben grabs him, elbows him in the face with his right, and punches him in the face with his left.

Possessed Man #19 grabs Ben by his wrist and Possessed Man #20 punches Ben in the stomach.

Possessed Man #19 quickly punches Ben in the face and Possessed Man #20 jumps on Ben's back.

Ben grabs Possessed Man #19 by the neck with his left and slices him.

Possessed Man #20 starts choking Ben and Ben stabs him twice.

Possessed Man #20 falls to the floor bleeding...

Another possessed, Possessed Man #21 spin kicks Ben in the face and Ben slices him with both knives in the chest.

EXT. UNDERGROUND CHURCH - SIDE OF CHURCH - SAME

Matthew recovers and Silas rushes over to him.

Matthew swings his sword at Silas and Silas blocks and pushes Matthew away.

Joseph picks up his sword and rushes toward Matthew.

His eyes glow blue as he runs...

Joseph quickly swings at Matthew's side, then his legs, and then at his face.

Matthew blocks each attack Joseph throws at him, though they get much stronger each time.

Joseph chops at Matthew and Matthew blocks.

Joseph pushes his sword toward Matthew and yells...

INT. UNDERGROUND CHURCH - FRONT ROOM

The twenty-second possessed man, O'reilly, 30, runs up to Eli and Eli grabs him, punches him with his left, then hits him with the staff in the side of his neck.

O'reilly flips and slams on the floor...

Possessed Man #23 runs up to Ben and jumps on his back.

Ben stabs his side twice.

Possessed Man #23 grabs Ben's brass knuckle knife from his right hand, rips it off, and tries to stab Ben.

Ben grabs him, and slams him on the ground.

He looks around for his other knife for a moment...

A female, Possessed Woman #8, rushes Eli, and Eli hits her in the side with his staff, and spin kicks her knocking her out.

Ben breathes heavily and looks at Eli.

Eli can't fully catch his breath either...

No possessed are around...

Possessed jump down from the upper level and rush David.

Eli looks over as six possessed men, Possessed Man #24, through #29, rush David.

David grabs #24 in a head lock, leans on him and kicks #25 in the face.

#24 wiggles out of David's grip, and swings at David.

David evades and punches him in the side of the face.

David drop kicks #26 and he falls...

David grapples #27, brings him to the floor and snaps his neck.

David jumps up, wraps his legs around #28's head, twists and breaks his neck.

#29 rushes David, and David rolls, and punches Possessed #29 in the gut.

EXT. UNDERGROUND CHURCH - SIDE - SAME

Joseph pushes his sword forward, and knocks Matthew down.

Matthew drops his sword and crawls toward it.

Joseph kicks Matthew in the gut as he crawls.

Matthew groans, and grabs his sword.

Joseph swings his sword at Matthew and Matthew blocks.

Joseph pushes down and Matthew rolls, and quickly stands.

Silas watches as blue flame comes out of Joseph's eyes...

INT. UNDERGROUND CHURCH - FRONT ROOM - SAME

Eli takes a step forward and Ben puts his hand in the way...

They both look at David fighting for a moment.

Eli looks at Ben and Ben shakes his head.

BEN
Let him go for a minute...

Henry, Tara, Martin and Calvin all jump from the upper level and approach David...

Henry rushes David and swings, but David moves out of the way, grabs Henry's shoulder with his left hand, and elbows him in the face with his right elbow.

Martin and Tara rush David.

Tara hits David in the back near his ribs...

David quickly spins, leg sweeps Tara, then turns and front kicks Martin.

David gets faster as each person comes at him...

Henry gets up, and heads toward David with Calvin.

David drops, holds himself up with one hand, and kicks Calvin and Henry in the face, then gets back on his feet.

Four possessed males, Possessed Man, #30 through #34, rush David.

David grabs #30, punches him in the gut, and powerfully headbutts him.

#31 swings at David, but David connects faster, with a quicker punch, then sweep kicks him and stomps on his chest.

David runs up and front kicks #32 in the chest, then spin kicks him in the throat.

#33 rushes and David takes off his gauntlet and throws it at #33, then runs up, twists and quickly spin kicks him in the face.

#34 kicks toward David, but he ducks and uppercuts him.

David looks at Ben and Eli as he picks up his gauntlet and puts it back on...

The brothers still try to catch their breath...

Ben nods, and Eli gives David a thumbs up...

EXT. UNDERGROUND CHURCH - SAME

Mammon tries to rip Angela away from his head, but Angela wraps her legs around his chest, and punches his arm twice.

Mammon groans, and moves his hand.

Angela keeps her right hand on Mammon's horn, and starts punching his head with her left.

Mammon rolls and stands...

INT. UNDERGROUND CHURCH - FRONT ROOM - SAME

David walks toward Ben and Eli.

O'reilly gets up from the floor, wipes blood from his mouth, and grabs Ben's brass knuckle knife from the ground.

David notices O'reilly.

                    DAVID
          Eli!

O'reilly stabs Eli in his side.

Eli grabs his side and groans.

Ben turns around, grabs O'reilly, rips the knife from his hands, slams him on the ground and stabs him.

>BEN
>
>Are you okay Eli?

>ELI
>
>Come on after all those hits from Mammon...
>I'll be fine.

>DAVID
>
>No, you could bleed out.

>ELI
>
>Let's just finish this.

David, Eli, and Ben look around.

>BEN
>
>Should we check there pulses?

David and Eli nod.

David, Eli, and Ben walk up to Possessed Man #7, #16, #17 and #18 as they squirm.

SERIES OF SHOTS as the three men check the possessed pulses.

Ben runs up and stabs Possessed #16, and #17.

Eli hits #18 in the head with his staff.

David smashes Possessed Man #7's chest with his gauntlets.

EXT. UNDERGROUND CHURCH - SAME

Angela stands, runs over to Mammon and punches him repeatedly with both hands.

Mammon grabs her.

Angela grabs his arm, pulls it away from her, kicks off his chest, jumps and yanks his arm off.

SIDE OF CHURCH

Matthew rushes Joseph and Joseph bats away Matthew's sword.

Joseph charges and stabs Matthew in the shoulder, then pins him down, and stabs the sword deep into the dirt.

He grabs Matthew's sword, stabs his other shoulder into the ground and grabs him by the throat with both hands.

Silas freezes and watches Joseph.

He closes his eyes and has a vision...

QUICK FLASH

EXT. CITY STREET - ALLEY - NIGHT

Martin and Calvin hold down Desta, while Matthew bites him in the neck...

Matthew backs away and Martin and Calvin let Desta go...

Desta holds his neck...

MATTHEW

You'll be fine...

Desta puts pressure on his neck and runs away..

Matthew wipes his mouth and walks toward the street...

BACK TO:

UNDERGROUND CHURCH - SIDE OF CHURCH - NIGHT

SILAS
Joseph stop!

Joseph continues to choke Matthew...

EXT. UNDERGROUND CHURCH - NIGHT

Ben, Eli, and David walk out.

Mammon looks at Angela as his arm drips out lava-like blood.

Angela runs up to Mammon, jumps on him, puts her feet on his chest, grabs his horns and starts to pull.

Mammon yells.

She rips off Mammon's head...

She drops Mammon's head, and Mammon falls over...

She rips out Mammon's heart, throws it on the ground, and bashes it.

CHURCH ENTRANCE

David looks at Silas and faintly hears him yell...

SILAS
Joseph! Let Matthew go!

DAVID
Come on let's go over to Silas!

                         ELI
                        Why?

                         DAVID
                 He wants to let Matthew go...

                          BEN
                        So what?

                         DAVID
                       So what!?

                          BEN
                 I already figured he would do that...

                         DAVID
                        What?!

                          ELI
              If it's one thing I know it's to trust Silas.

Ben stretches and sits down.

David runs over to Joseph and Silas.

                         SILAS
                 We're going to need him Joseph!

Silas tries to run up to Joseph and a large blue orb surrounds him.

Silas quickly stops before running into the orb.

ON BEN AND ELI

                          ELI
                  Holy shit! What's that?

Eli runs over towards Joseph...

Ben stands...

ON JOSEPH

Joseph continues to choke Matthew.

> SILAS
> Stop! You don't have to kill him...

Joseph ignores Silas...

> DAVID
> What are you talking about?!

> SILAS
> He needs to stop!

> DAVID
> Why!?

Eli runs up and looks at Joseph through the orb...

Ben walks up and Joseph looks at everyone...

> ELI
> We took out everyone Joe... He has nothing...
> You can let go...

Joseph notices Eli's wound...

He stops choking Matthew, and the blue orb goes away...

Matthew struggles to get the swords out of his shoulders.

He stands, and starts to run away...

> DAVID
> We're seriously letting him go!?

> SILAS
> We already achieved more than we wanted today.

David shakes his head.

Matthew leaps a few long jumps.

Angela leaps out of nowhere and kicks Matthew in the back...

Matthew flies forward and smashes into a rock...

ON SILAS

> JOSEPH
> What's she doing?

> SILAS
> She just attacked him... I didn't make her...

> JOSEPH
> What the hell do you mean?

> SILAS
> I haven't practiced mind control much, so I haven't fully got it figured out...

ON ANGELA

Matthew leaps into the air.

Angela jumps and grabs him.

> MATTHEW
> No! Get off me!

Angela grabs Matthew's shoulder and headbutts him.

ON SILAS

> SILAS
> I'll have her stop in a moment... he'll be fine...
> no harm in one final scare before he goes.

Silas focuses on Angela and squints his eyes...

ON ANGELA

> MATTHEW
> Get off me!

Angela slams Matthew on the ground...

Matthew stands up and looks at Angela...

She stands still...

He quickly runs toward the underground tunnel.

ON SILAS

Silas looks at Joseph.

> SILAS
> What happened to you just now?

> JOSEPH
> Honestly Silas... I can't really explain... just rage.

David starts walking away...

Eli and Ben walk up.

ELI

Can one of you give me a lift?

Silas looks at Joseph and nods.

JOSEPH

Alright come on.

Eli puts his arm over Joseph's shoulder and Joseph flies off.

They fly passed David.

Ben walks up to Silas and puts his hand on his shoulder.

BEN

I'm sorry Silas...

SILAS

Thank you Ben... but I've had a long, long time to grieve... Go ahead... I have to say goodbye to her for now...

Ben nods and walks away.

EXT. FORREST AREA - DAY

The sun is rising up but is still behind the mountains...

Joseph and Eli fly over the trees.

They see Matthew running.

He looks up at them, turns, and runs into the woods.

ON MATTHEW

Matthew runs for a moment through the trees...

                    DANA
          Matthew!

Matthew notices Dana and runs up to her.

                    DANA
          Come with me.

Dana closes her eyes, and puts her hands together...

A dark portal opens up in front of them and they jump in.

UNDERGROUND TUNNEL ENTRANCE

Ben climbs out, notices David walking ahead of him with his hands in his pockets, and runs up to him.

Ben puts his hand on David's shoulder as they walk.

INT. UNDERGROUND CHURCH - SIDE OF CHURCH - SAME

Silas stands with Angela near the tomb.

He grabs her shoulders and looks into her eyes.

                    SILAS
          I'm going to find a way to get this thing out of
          you... I promise.

He hugs her for a moment...

One of her hands slowly touches his elbow.

Silas stops hugging her and looks at her for a moment...

She looks at him with a dead stare...

Silas looks at the ground... then looks at Mammon's corpse...

INT. LAWRENCE'S PLANE - DAY

Ben sits by Eli...

Eli holds a towel on his side and looks out the window...

Joseph and Silas sit near David and Lawrence sits by himself across from them leaning his head back, resting.

INT. BLACK CAR - DAY

Inside the car Ben sits with Eli in the back...

Terry drives.

> BEN
> Are you sure about this?

The car pulls up to a hospital.

> ELI
> I have to...

Eli gets out.

> BEN
> We'll figure it out alright?

Eli nods and shuts the door...

INT. HOSPITAL - EMERGENCY ROOM - NIGHT (LATER)

The room is packed with people waiting.

Eli walks in and limps to the counter.

The lady behind the counter, Doris, 40, types on her computer, ignoring Eli for a moment...

She looks at Eli, who is beaten, dirty, and bloody.

Eli holds his wound, that has a fresh bandage...

                    DORIS
          Oh my goodness! One moment sir.

She presses a button in front of her several times.

                    ELI
          Thank you.

Two men walk out and up to Eli.

He puts his arms over both men and they help him walk.

INT. LAWRENCE'S MANSION - LIVING ROOM - NIGHT

The living room is large with high vaulted ceilings and a large window that peers onto the front lawn.

Silas and Joseph sit on a couch.

Lawrence sits on an arm chair, and Ben and David stand, leaning against a wall...

                    BEN
          I don't think he's safe there... They're gonna
          come after him.

> LAWRENCE
> Hopefully not, but I called my military friend...
> I'm waiting for a call back...

> SILAS
> We had to take him.

> DAVID
> We can't fight our way out of this.

INT. LAWRENCE'S MANSION - OFFICE - DAY (LATER)

Lawrence sits at his desk.

Daryl, 60, sits across from Lawrence wearing a collard shirt and slacks.

> DARYL
> Okay Lawrence what is so important that we
> couldn't have just spoke on the phone?

Silas, and Ben walk into the room from the hall.

Daryl jumps out of his seat.

> SILAS
> My name is Silas, this is Ben.

> DARYL
> What the hell Lawrence!?

> LAWRENCE
> Government officials stormed their house...
> thankfully they got away. We need a meeting
> with higher officials... I know that you have to
> report any inside threats you learn about...

DARYL

Are you two a threat?

SILAS

They think we are but I assure you, we're not...

Daryl relaxes, nods...

DARYL

Alright then... I'll help you guys get a meeting...

EXT. MILITARY BASE - NIGHT

Lawrence's plane lands in a cargo area, and David, Lawrence, Joseph, Silas, and Ben get out...

INT. LARGE OFFICE - NIGHT

A military man, Merrill, 50, sits behind a desk.

Two guards stand on the sides of the desk, carrying M4 rifles...

Silas and Joseph stand near the desk, Ben leans on a wall near them, and David and Lawrence stand close to the door...

MERRILL

The operation to attack your cabin was approved due to it being a matter of National Security...

SILAS

What do you mean?

MERRILL

After hearing your story we know now that we may have been looking for Matthew... I've gone through the files... there was an investigation...

There were tons of reports of sightings, even
photos... of you Silas...

> BEN
> (to Silas)
> Come on man...

> SILAS
> After hundreds of years there's gonna be some
> photos snapped...

Joseph smirks...

> MERRILL
> There were also a lot of reports of people being
> bitten and killed by... what seemed to be a
> vampire.

> SILAS
> So you found me... and thought I had done
> everything?

Merrill nods...

> BEN
> Matthew doesn't have wings though...

> MERRILL
> We know that now... but we don't have any
> photos of Matthew... Not to mention Silas... you
> were easy to find...

> SILAS
> Are you still going to investigate us?

MERRILL

Well yes... but rest assured we will not attack you guys again... and the man from your group that is in the hospital is safe...

BEN

For the record me and my brother were just defending ourselves...

MERRILL

We completely understand... Those men went on that mission voluntarily and they knew about you two, so there's nothing you need to worry about...

BEN

Okay...

MERRILL

Just so you guys know, we're planning on holding a press conference acknowledging your group... and the existence of... angels, giants, and vampires.

Silas looks at everyone and they all nod...

SILAS

I think we're all okay with that...

Ben smiles and looks at Silas...

INT. HOSPITAL - ROOM - DAY

Eli lies on a bed asleep while a doctor sits next to him filling out paperwork... After a moment Eli wakes up...

                          DOCTOR
          Hi there...

                          ELI
          Hello...

                          DOCTOR
          Surgery went fine... You must have God
          watching your back... you were stabbed right
          near your femoral artery.

The doctor walks out.

Eli stands, and walks over to his clothes, folded on a chair.

INT. BAR - DAY - LATER

The bar is medium sized with a freshly polished wooden counter top...

Several men sitting at the bar, watch a TV mounted on the wall.

ON TV

PRESS CONFERENCE ROOM

HEADLINE READS: "GOVERNMENT ACKNOWLEDGES
GROUP OF FRIENDLY SUPER HUMANS."

A man in a suit, Bob, 50, stands in front of a podium with several
microphones on it.

                          BOB
          We met with them and they do not want people
          to be afraid.

CAMERA FLASHES HIT BOB

A reporter raises his hand...

> REPORTER
> Does the government have a name for the group yet?

> BOB
> Well so far, we have been calling them... The Superiors.

INT. LAWRENCE'S MANSION - LIVING ROOM - DAY

David sits on a chair, and Ben and Eli sit on a couch...

Joseph stands looking out the window to the front lawn...

The TV plays the press conference...

> ELI
> The whole world knows about us...

> JOSEPH
> What do we do now?...

> BEN
> I guess we could all go home...

EXT. LAWRENCE'S MANSION - KITCHEN - NIGHT

Lawrence, Silas, Ben, Eli, Joseph, and David are all in the kitchen.

Lawrence sits at the kitchen table next to Silas, and Ben and Eli sit across from them.

Joseph stands near them, and David stands a bit further back.

Ben and Eli both have a paper plate with a grilled cheese on it in front of them.

Joseph holds a sub sandwich, and David eats a plate of rice, with black beans and corn mixed in, on the counter.

                    BEN
          And then me and Eli looked at David, and that
          dude was on fire man... We just let him go.

Everyone smiles except for David...

                    ELI
          YOU said let him be, I was ready to fight until
          my body gave out.

                    BEN
          Me too but he handled it just fine.

Silas looks over at David quietly eating...

EXT. LAWRENCE'S MANSION - DRIVEWAY - NIGHT

The black car sits in the driveway running.

Everyone walks out.

Joseph waves and flies off...

Ben and David stand near the front door.

                    BEN
          I saw you get hit by Matthew

David... How did it not phase you?

DAVID
I'm not sure...

BEN
You also took that hit from me...

DAVID
Maybe... I don't know... Maybe my instincts were able to somehow help me absorb the punch... but... something tells me I can't do stuff like that too much...

BEN
Alright... Well it's been real man...

David nods and shakes Ben's hand...

Ben and Eli wave, walk up to the car and get inside...

The car drives off...

Silas and Lawrence shake hands.

SILAS
Thank you again Lawrence.

LAWRENCE
Yeah don't mention it.

Silas looks at David and walks over to him.

DAVID
Alright Silas... see you...

Silas and David shake his hands.

SILAS
Thanks for everything David...

DAVID
Hey Silas... Why didn't you know Angela would be part of the plan?

SILAS
I wasn't sure at first about getting her to help... Once we got there and fought Mammon I knew...

DAVID
Why weren't you sure at first?

SILAS
The visions... they're not always easy to interpret... I'm constantly thinking of Angela... so I wouldn't know if what is going through my head is a thought, or if I'm being shown something...

DAVID
She probably could've done everything by herself...

SILAS
That wouldn't have been a good plan David... We still needed to be there to make sure everything got handled right. Also... I have no idea how long the mind control works for... I've barely used it in the past... I really don't know enough about it... I don't even know if it'll work again....

David nods...

SILAS

Next time... maybe you could try what you did with her again... How did you even do that David?...

DAVID

I don't know... I've been having a recurring dream for a while... where I'm... in a room with a lion... and I get it to be calm... I thought of that when I heard her roar, so I thought of the dream...

Silas nods and pauses for a moment...

SILAS

Are you still upset about Matthew?

DAVID

We let a murderous vampire go Silas...

SILAS

We may need him...

DAVID

He's evil. We can't trust him...

SILAS

When Joseph was about to kill Matthew... I was shown a vision of him feeding on someone, and letting them go... If that vision came to me at THAT time... I have to assume it meant something...

DAVID

Why didn't you just choose to ignore the vision?

SILAS

People know what the right move is, and do the opposite too often. Why do that? I don't know why The Lord wants Matthew alive, but maybe it's because he can do some good.

DAVID

Why did you say we might need him? Do you know something is gonna happen? A potential future threat?

SILAS

David... just know that there are many things that could happen in the future on Earth...

David nods...

DAVID

Alright Silas... Take care...

SILAS

You too... I'll see you David...

David nods and watches Silas jump, and fly off...

THE END